Andrew Jackson Davis, Della E. Davis

Starnos

Quotations from the Inspired Writings of Andrew Jackson Davis

Andrew Jackson Davis, Della E. Davis

Starnos
Quotations from the Inspired Writings of Andrew Jackson Davis

ISBN/EAN: 9783337407742

Printed in Europe, USA, Canada, Australia, Japan

Cover: Foto ©Andreas Hilbeck / pixelio.de

More available books at **www.hansebooks.com**

STARNOS:

QUOTATIONS FROM THE INSPIRED WRITINGS

OF

ANDREW JACKSON DAVIS,

Seer of the Harmonial Philosophy.

SELECTED AND EDITED

By DELLA E. DAVIS, M.D.

"We visited the summit of Starnos,—the Mount of Light,—south of the beautiful Lake Mornia.—*Penetralia,* p. 261.

BOSTON:

COLBY & RICH, PUBLISHERS,

9 BOSWORTH STREET,

1891.

INTRODUCTION.

Many years ago it was my good fortune to become acquainted with the writings of Andrew Jackson Davis on the Spiritual Philosophy, or Harmonial Philosophy,—a title that is better known and associated with the author's name and works, by those who read and know them. To the persons and powers which prevailed, and were the means of introducing me to a knowledge and perception of their mission and great value to the world, I can never cease to feel the most profound gratitude. The principles and teachings embodied in these writings were to *me*, as I believe they have been to many others, and what they cannot fail to prove to all who honestly and faithfully seek for light through them, a Savior who opened to my view a new heaven and a new earth,—an unfailing Fountain full of "jets of new meaning."

Although reared from early youth with an atheistic view of life, with its accompanying unbelief in any personal responsibility regarding the soul's future, yet I also inherited an ardent admiration for the true and the beautiful. I have naturally a profound reverence and love for the sublime and wonderful in all the manifestations of nature. My *spirit*, therefore, was not only ready but felt eager to break through the encrusting materialism, and to recognize more perfectly the inner meanings and import of life. I needed some thing or some one who might show me the true and sure way out from the night of mental errors, and the gloom of *ignorance*, into the full and blessed light of day.

Modern Spiritualism came to me as a great joy, assisting me over many rough and barren places in my mental journeyings. It proved to me the fact of a continued individual life beyond this body-bound earthly existence; that the event termed death is in reality a birth into a higher and better conditioned life; and that those who pass beyond this portal can and do return to earth, and with signs and messages give proof of their identity and love. But the Harmonial Philosophy, which embodies all that is good and true in all *isms*, was to me a still greater blessing. *It* held aloft for me the Beacon Torch which guided me out of *all* my former skepticism into the perfect faith, and imparted an ever growing knowledge of the principles underlying and governing the methods and processes of all existence. Amid the storms of severe and almost engulfing personal experiences; when the waters of life were made bitter as gall with mental conflicts and doubts; "through dark nights of sorrow mid anguish and tears"; when confidence in human and divine love grew weak and feeble because of *ignorance;* when hope well nigh hid its face, and faith most needed a savior; then the light of the Harmonial Philosophy illumined the gloom and desolation with revealings of God's eternal justice, love, and wisdom, working always for the redemption and ultimate perfection of all.

I could now see that life's disciplines were the chisels in the hands of a Divine Artist, who was carving from the rock of ages beautiful forms and fashioning them in his own likeness and image; and that we as human beings can, by living purely and healthfully, soonest comprehend and realize his secret intentions,— the evolution and

establishment of the Kingdom of Heaven in the
human heart. Many years ago, before any personal acquaintance with Mr. Davis, I was wont
to call myself a disciple of the "Harmonial Philosophy," which term to many was an unknown
quantity without any significance. When read-
ing and studying its volumes I often met with
passages which to me embodied so much of wisdom and practical worth that I would be inspired with the wish and hope that some person
might be moved to select from out of the many
a sufficient number of paragraphs to make a
convenient and inexpensive book, so that any-
one not having access to the writings on these
spiritual themes might read the inspired passages.

One day, "in the gloaming," before the evening lamp was lighted, and while reclining for a
little rest and meditation, I received an impression, which was imperative, that *I* was the
person to commence and accomplish this com-
pilation. Receiving the approval and encour-
agement of the author, I almost immediately
set to work to make selections and to prepare
them for publication. The result is this little
volume, STARNOS,— my rosary of pearls as I

call it,— which is tenderly and affectionately extended to the world, with the heart prayer that its contents may convey to all who read it the light and solace which every mind and heart constantly needs. It has certainly been a labor of love on my part, and if any hungering soul can from its pages find the true comforter, then my reward will be sure, and soul satisfying.

Greetings to all! with the love and blessing of the author and compiler.

BOSTON, MASS., 1891.

STARNOS.

A.

ARABULA.

Arabula is the perfect, the eternal, love-light and light-love of the universe; and when it dwelleth in our superior consciousness, we not only love *it* without fear, but also love tenderly all humanity, and even the least and lowest things of the earth, and the earth itself, and likewise all things in the starry heavens, with a love that is unutterable, mysterious, sublime, and blossoming with happiness.— Arabula, p. 110.

AUTHORITY.

The authority of the Harmonial Philosophy is Truth; it is not based upon the Revelations of "Davis," but upon the Revelations of Nature.— Gt. Har. Vol. 3, p. 375.

Nature, the great exponent of God; and Reason, the great exponent of Nature,—these are the supreme Authority upon all things which pertain to man and his Maker.— Gt. Har. Vol. 3, p. 390.

ASPIRATION.

To be like heaven let us aspire to heaven. —Gt. Har. Vol. 2, p. 180.

Aspiration is the true basis of every true idea concerning goodness, greatness, and Deity.— Gt. Har. Vol. 2, p. 154.

Aspiration humanizes, spiritualizes, and nobly defines every modification and tendency of that internal promethean fire which ever burns in the soul.— Gt. Har. Vol. 2, p. 154.

ATMOSPHERES.

There is a *spiritual* atmosphere *within* the material atmosphere. The soul feeds on the one, the body upon the other, until, by a refining process, they blend into *one*, whereby the spirit is made to increase in substance.— Gt. Har. Vol. 4, p. 54.

ASSOCIATION.

Particles of matter are associated according to their shape, their size, and their temperament. . . . One shape and temperament of atoms, for example, will be attracted only to granite; another to quartz; another to limestone; another to iron, or silver, or copper, or gold; . . . another to animals; another to the human form; another to the sun; . . . another to trees; another to the human soul,— all, in accordance with the degree of the harmony of shape, size, and temperament (or attractions) of the composing atoms.— Gt. Har. Vol. 4, p. 277.

ANGELS.

As the Goddess of music takes down her lute, touches its silver chords, and sets the summer melodies of nature to words; so an angel from the Spirit Land comes to us in our profoundest slumber and gently awakens our highest faculties to the finest thought and serenest contemplation.— Gt. Har. Vol. 3, p. 317.

ATTRACTION.

Attraction is that law which associates and consociates, which joins and conjoins, atoms with life, life with organization, organization with intelligence. Therefore, this attraction is the *love-law* of all organization ; the same in the physical world as in the spiritual. . . . The coming together of atoms conjugally elected,— that is, according to their inherent relations and essential affinities,— makes the organal phenomena of field and forest, of sea and sky.— Gt. Har. Vol. 4, p. 277.

ARISTOCRACIES.

One-third of the earth's population are bound by the hand of disease, merely because they are uneducated, inferiorly conditioned, and unjustly treated by the exclusiveness of classes and aristocracies.— Nat. Div. Rev., p. 698.

ACHIEVEMENTS.

The greatest of achievements and the holiest of demonstrations is the actual passage of private love-messages to and fro between this rock-bound stormy shore and that vernal margin just beyond the floating clouds.— His. and Phil. of Evil, p. 46.

APPROBATION.

Speak boldly and fearlessly your earnest and serious convictions, and Nature will smile upon you with her divine approbations; the angels will rejoice, and the Divine Mind will bless your mind with celestial knowledge.— Nat. Div. Rev., p. 714.

ALLEGIANCE.

Perfect righteousness in one's allegiance and conduct to whatsoever is good, true, divine, and beautiful — to the pure, just, loving, wise, and merciful — is a principle of the *spirit.*— Gt. Har. Vol. 5, p. 83.

AGENTS.

Unseen powers within the spirit are certain to be silently aided in the performance of good deeds by vigilant agents of mercy who daily move through the atmosphere of the world upon the silvery wings of love.— Temple, p. 361.

ADVANCEMENT.

When the soul is sufficiently advanced in strength, it discards its cradle,— it steps boldly from the threshold of the tabernacle in which it was born,— and treads the interminable paths of infinitude like an angel of God.— Gt. Har. Vol. 3, p. 64.

ANGER.

Impatient, angry tones never did the heart good, but plenty of evil.— Fountain, p. 146.

AFFECTION.

Love is the source of quantity in a person. There is great fullness of life where there is great affection, which flows out of love's fountain.— Heavenly Home, p. 25.

ATTRACTION.

Noble sentiments and profound feelings of human nature *attract* appreciable influences from the invisible sphere whence emanates " every good and perfect gift."— Memoranda, p. 31.

ARGUMENT.

Argument is the kitchen work of the mind. Wisdom never argues; it states principles, and gives methods. It believes that nothing can be taught; everything can be developed. — Gt. Har. Vol. 4, p. 38.

AFFECTION.

Rightly seen, everything in nature is a wise and special expression of divine affection. — Fountain, p. 21.

ABSTINENCE.

If you cannot sleep well, abstain from food and warm drink subsequent to *four* o'clock in the afternoon.— Inner Life, p. 383.

AFFLICTION.

There is almost always a subduing, refining, and spiritualizing influence emanating from the seeming evils of physical affliction. — Gt. Har. Vol. 1, p. 145.

AFFECTION.

Every private affection throws out an atmosphere. Whatever your predominating love may be, it emits an atmosphere which winds itself about your person.— Death and After Life, p. 134.

ASSOCIATION.

Everything has its own peculiar atmosphere, and consequently its specific and necessary association.— Nat. Div. Rev., p. 147.

ASPIRATIONS.

The eternal spirit of *self-preservation* throbs mightily and supremely at the very heart of all individual aspiration.— Gt. Har.   Vol. 5, p. 396.

AMBITION.

A high, pure purpose, be it remembered, is possible only to *spirit*. Ambition is earthly; aspiration is spiritual.— Phil. Spiritual Intercourse, p. 353.

ATTRACTION.

Attraction is that principle of *Love* which perpetually fills and harmoniously beats in, and from, the two united hearts and heads of Father God and Mother Nature.— Temple, p. 108.

ACTIVITIES.

Activity is the wealth of the world, and the use and destiny of man.— Nat. Div. Rev., p. 690.

AUTHORITY.

No mind ever received truth until it divested itself of *pride, arrogance*, and attachment to *human* Authority.—Gt. Har. Vol. 2, p. 134.

ANTIQUITY.

Antiquity is a poor authority, being characteristically shrouded in the winding-sheet of error, superstition, and misapprehensions of the commonest facts.— Gt. Har. Vol. 5, p. 134.

ATMOSPHERES.

Every human soul is surrounded with an atmosphere, more or less pure and influential. This atmosphere is an emanation from the individual, just as flowers exhale their fragrance.— Gt. Har. Vol. 1, p. 286.

ANNIHILATION.

There is nothing capable of annihilation in all the realms of Infinitude.— Penetralia, p. 115.

ARABULA.

The sensibilities and sentiments and aspirations and apprehensions of the superior powers of mind are the voices of Arabula.— Arabula, p. 371.

APPLAUSE.

If you are good, if you are great, the secret will be found out. Do not mourn a moment over the blindness and non-appreciation of your fellowmen.— Beyond the Valley, p. 380.

ARBITRATION.

In any troubles and misunderstandings which you may experience as arising from your relations with others, do not forget the Friendly Board of Arbitration,— *Love, Sincerity, Truth!*— Beyond the Valley, p. 141.

ANGELS.

Justice, honor, truth, love, reverence, are the " holy angels " that guard the inner temple.— Gt. Har. Vol. 5, p. 228.

AFFINITIES.

The mind's internal affinities are inter-cohesive, and stronger than all extrinsic attractions.— Gt. Har. Vol. 5, p. 326.

ART.

Art refines and spiritualizes the feelings, and opens the interior senses to the more glorious perception and appreciation of nature's beauties.— Gt. Har. Vol. 2, p. 87.

ANALYSIS.

Self-analysis is indispensable to spiritual progress. . . . Self-discipline, self-confession of faults, and self-harmonization will flow out of the *analysis*, as streams flow from the fountain.— Gt. Har. Vol. 2, p. 177.

AIMS.

Aim for Peace and Justice; think of a better world that changes not.— Inner Life, p. 148.

ARMOR.

That mind that loves truth more than any other thing is clothed in the armor of Heaven. — Inner Life, p. 42.

ABUSES.

Abuses and perversions creep into every exalted sphere of human interest; and the celestial flower-like loveliness and exquisite delicacy of spiritual intercourse cannot claim exemption.— Temple, p. 244.

B.

BEAUTY.

A body full of virtuous health — of harmony deserved — is a form of holy beauty.— Harbinger of Health, p. 34.

BOOKS.

We are all authors. We write books. Every day opens a fresh leaf in some heart, on which we trace some line of thought,— make some impression theron which can never fade away.— Har. Man., p. 155.

BIRTH.

To be born, to come into the world, to exist, to grow, to attain the full stature, and live forever,— this is indeed sacred, wonderful, awful, attractive, beautiful.— Gen. and Eth. of Conj. Love, p. 61.

BONDAGE.

Strive by will-power and inward growth to live less in bondage to circumstances.— Hist. and Phil. of Evil, p. 220.

BEAUTY.

Beauty is the prophecy of the perfection which is in store for *each* in the growth of time.— Eth. of Conj. Love, p. 84.

BIGOTRY.

Creeds cannot withstand the pulverizing advancement of positive science. Bigotry cannot set back the on-rolling tides of universal Brotherhood.— Fountain, p. 74.

BLESSINGS.

Secure ye first the kingdom of harmony in material things,—in diet, activities, dress, etc., — then all the innumerable blessings of virtue and progress shall be added.— Answers to Questions, p. 39.

BLESSINGS.

Looking afar for a blessing, instead of just at your feet, where the richest diamond lies hidden in the coarse sand, illustrates the difference between a fool and a philosopher.— Our Heavenly Home, p. 254.

BEAUTY.

Beauty is a condition, but it can only be recognized and appreciated by a corresponding internal state or attribute in the individual. — Gt. Har. Vol. 2, p. 152.

When Nature is bathed in the glowing and glorious emanations from the source of all light and life,— and when every tree, every bird, and every flower, is drinking in and breathing forth the soft luxuriance of spiritual hues,— then the mind cannot but perceive and realize something of the loveliness and magnificence of the Second Sphere to which all mankind are journeying.— Gt. Har. Vol. 1, p. 280.

BROTHERHOOD.

That mind which is pure, and properly educated in the ways of wisdom, can only recognize mankind as a Brotherhood.— Nat. Div. Rev., p. 575.

BEAUTY.

Fraternal love is the companion, the *conjugal* companion, of the attribute of Beauty. This love inspires, and Beauty is her manifestation.— Gt. Har. Vol. 2, p. 153.

BOOKS.

Forest trees full of singing birds are the chapters of good books with their white leaves. — Beyond the Valley, p. 279.

A book is your best friend when it compels you to think, disenthralls your reason, enkindles your hopes, vivifies your imagination, dispels the darkness of materialism, and makes easier all the burdens of your daily life.— Beyond the Valley, p. 279.

BLESSINGS.

All things are blessings only as they come and go when needed.— Penetralia, p. 458.

BENEFITS.

Whatever increases the sum of human knowledge, and augments the joys of the human soul, is beneficial to the world.— Penetralia, p. 328.

BEATITUDES.

The power to rise up into the Divine beatitudes arises from the just and generous performances of deeds of kindness, of mercy, of justice, of love.— Memoranda, p. 314.

BODY.

The human body was made to develop the human spirit.— Gt. Har.   Vol. 1, p. 189.

The body is the mold into which the "*elixir* of immortality" is run.— Inner Life, p. 406.

BROTHERHOOD.

The soul desires fellowship with its kind.
Fraternal affection inspires the desire for
universal association. Its magic word is
" Brotherhood." . . . In its natural state of
action it responds heartily to the golden rule
or gospel synopsis,— *love to man; love to
God.*— Gt. Har. Vol. 4, p. 78.

BELIEF.

Believe not a truth because it was believed
and taught before you lived, but because it *is*
truth, leading the mind onward and upward
to higher spheres of grandeur and beauty.—
Nat. Div. Rev., p. 433.

Any belief that has a tendency to destroy
the natural benevolence of a noble mind, or
to restrict its movements and circumscribe its
sympathies and affections, . . . is indeed not
worthy of the most contracted place in the human affections, or among the approved tenets
of the judgment.— Nat. Div. Rev., p. 491.

BABYHOOD.

The babyhood of the whole human race, like the infant state of the individual man, is characterized by physical weakness and mental simplicity.— Hist. and Phil. of Evil, p. 13.

C.

CREATION.

Creation is a beautiful sermon, terminating with a grand, glowing, glorious conclusion,— the human Soul.— Inner Life, p. 66.

CHARACTER.

The mind and its affections grow to resemble in shape and feeling that upon which they constantly feed; and from the structure and affections of the mind we derive and establish "character."— Fountain, p. 36.

CONSCIENCE.

The Kingdom of Heaven is within you, and *Conscience* is the Divinity that rules therein.— Gt. Har. Vol. 1, p. 156.

CAPABILITIES.

The Spirit is capable, by its power, of subduing itself and the various creations beneath it in nature.— Gt. Har. Vol. 2, p. 152.

CHARITY.

Charity is fraternal justice. . . . . No man is justified in returning evil for evil, but good only under all circumstances and to all humanity.— Gt. Har. Vol. 5, p. 96.

CULTIVATION.

When man becomes highly cultivated in his affections and intellect, all elements will be invested with a diviner meaning, even to the recognition of the Supreme Being in their silvery depths.— Gt. Har. Vol. 3, p. 238.

CHARACTER.

Perfection and truthfulness of character are the secret intentions of Nature.— Gt. Har. Vol. 5, p. 15.

CIRCUMSTANCES.

Influences and circumstances which sway human feeling and modify judgment, are but the wire-pullings and mathematical calculations of positive prescience.— Gt. Har. Vol. 5, p. 152.

CULTURE.

Happiness is the end of all human desire and endeavor, and spiritual culture is the agency by which it may be obtained.— Gt. Har. Vol. 2, p. 174.

The law and method of spiritual culture require the following: *Be contented with the Past, and with all it has brought you.* Be thankful for the Present, and for all you have. Be patient for the Future, and for all it promises to bring you.— Gt. Har. Vol. 2, p. 174.

CAUSES.

God is the cause — Nature is the effect —
Man is the ultimate.— Inner Life, p. 53.

CONSTITUTION.

The constitution of the human spirit prohibits the possibility of its loving and cherish-
ing unqualified error.— Gt. Har. Vol. 1,
p. 240.

CIRCUMSTANCES.

A true Harmonial Philosopher — a real,
spiritual, living soul — can rise up and live a
higher life in the midst of his circumstances.
— Thoughts Concerning Religion, p. 177.

CONSOLATION.

Remember in your darkest hours that there
are those in the bending skies that *love* you!
Strive to do well then, to be a true Beautiful
Woman, to be a pure Harmonial Man ; and
the higher worlds will baptize you in its sweet
and living waters.— Gt. Har. Vol. 4, p. 181.

COMMANDMENT.

Under all circumstances keep an even mind.
— Magic Staff, p. 263.

CORRECTNESS.

Correct speaking, like good dancing, comes by frequent practice under the guidance of wise instructors.— Eth. of Conj. Love, p. 112.

CIRCULATION.

In the human body there is a vitalic circulation; so is there a circulation of vital forces between the spiritual world and the several planets.— Gt. Har. Vol. 5, p. 414.

COMMUNION.

Opening of the interior *feeling* to a full and free communion with eternal principles is the only door, swinging on golden hinges, which admits the traveler to the immediate presence of the infinite Father and Mother.— Heavenly Home, p. 21.

CHEERFULNESS.

To be cheerfully reconciled to the unavoidable, to be satisfied with the best you can be and do, is wise and beautiful.— Eth. of Conj. Love, p. 126.

CONDITIONS.

When man shall convert bad physical and social *conditions* into good and healthy *influences*, the moral wilderness will blossom as the rose, and the lion and lamb of the interior man will lie down together in peace.— Gt. Har. Vol. 3, p. 26.

CHARACTER.

The harmonial formation of character — *in harmony with the principles of Universal Love and Distributive Justice* — is the only security against temporal unhappiness and future disturbances. . . . Harmony of character and loveliness of disposition unfold gradually from unwavering efforts to acquire them.— Penetralia, p. 290.

CHEERFULNESS.

Cheerfulness is an *all-healing medicine* prepared in the laboratory of the gods.— Heavenly Home, p. 56.

CONTEMPLATION.

There is nothing too free, too stupendous, too magnificent, or *too holy*, for human contemplation.— Gt. Har. Vol. 2, p. 255.

CIRCUMSTANCES.

As is the moistened clay in the hands of the potter, so is individual man in the wheel of the most positive circumstances.— Gt. Har. Vol. 5, p. 247.

CAUSES.

It is a self-evident proposition that all external effects must spring from invisible causes. . . . In everything the ideal begets the actual; the invisible, the visible; the principle, the outward manifestation.— Gt. Har. Vol. 3, p. 56.

CRITICISM.

Healthy criticism is the best mental fertilizer because it plows up the soil of thought and prepares it for the best seed-grains of truth.— Answers to Questions, p. 249.

CORRESPONDENCE.

Between inward bodies and principles there is invariably a well-defined outward correspondence. . . . The objective violet imparts to the mental canvas a likeness of its own image.— Gt. Har. Vol. 5, p. 165.

CONTEMPLATION.

It is very spiritualizing to one's superior sensibilities, and love of beauty and harmony, to ascend some enchanting elevation above the highest tree-tops, and from that lofty solitude contemplate and absorb the impressions imparted by the soft, hazy, indefiniteness of a vastly extended landscape.— Heavenly Home, p. 100.

CHURCHES.

The free church of the future will be the Sanctuary of Reason,— dispensing spiritual and natural Truths to a free and happy audience.— His. and Phil. of Evil, p. 102.

COMMANDMENTS.

If you wish to be truly and steadfastly loved, see to it that you do not deform your spiritual nature.— Gt. Har. Vol. 4, p. 222.

Prepare yourselves to love one another. . . . Become lovable.   Let each become lovely as possible. . . . Love is an attribute, spontaneous, like genius, obeying no laws save its own.— Gt. Har.   Vol. 4, p. 221.

Let your minds be calm ; put confidence in the divine laws of your being ; obey them religiously ; and youth and beauty will glow from every face,— and, without trying, you will "love one another."— Gt. Har. Vol. 4, p. 222.

CONSOLATION.

True and lasting consolation — also true
and abiding happiness — comes from the daily
doing of *right*, which is your *duty*. This is
the everlasting guide to peace.— Beyond the
Valley, p. 391.

COMPENSATIONS.

Pleasure, happiness, joy, blessedness, bliss,
— these spiritual sensations will come as com-
pensations for duty done, for work performed,
for loyalty to the omnipresent spirit of the
ever-wise, ever-loving Arabula.— Beyond the
Valley, p. 20.

CHEERFULNESS.

Never be depressed ; but be cheerful — be
joyful — be exceedingly glad — even though
death is knocking at your door — for there is
nothing to hate, to shun, to fear, or to deplore,
in any department of Nature, or in the wide
sanctuary of the Living, Divine Mind.— Gt.
Har. Vol. 1, p. 442.

COUNTERPARTS.

Deity and Nature are counterparts ; they are husband and wife, father and mother, wisdom and love.— Thoughts on Religion, p. 91.

CONSTELLATIONS.

The stellar constellations are chords in the harp upon which Mother Nature sounds the music of her everlasting love of God.— Beyond the Valley, p. 320.

CHARACTER.

The higher the development of character the more impreguable does the individual become to the causes and afflictions of evil.— Answers to Questions, p. 188.

CLEANLINESS.

There is something *more* than beauty of form, face, and manners ; that something is personal purity and cleanliness.— Eth. of Conj. Love, p. 84.

CHARACTER.

Go deep into human character, and you will find a diamond inheritance, pure and imperishable.— Penetralia, p. 404.

CONSCIOUSNESS.

Consciousness is irresistable, absolute, irreversible, and beyond controversy. It is that which you accept without question. You live in it because it is yourself.— Answers to Questions, p. 17.

CONVENTIONS.

Conventions, conducted with magnanimity and virtue of purpose, will accomplish much good towards the unfolding of universal principles.— Thoughts on Religion, p. 21.

Conventions are useful only as ploughs are good for the soil,— they turn up *new ground*, break away poisonous weeds, and demolish old stumps, for the subsequent planting of good seed.— Thoughts on Religion, p. 15.

COURAGE.

We need more independence of soul,— not impudence or arrogance, but strength enough, courage enough, to do the bidding of our instincts, and rebuke the wrong which timidity generates.— Harmonial Man, p. 148.

COMPASSION.

It is good to feel that every soul contains the same elements of energy and intellect. Such a conviction will inspire us with a philosophical compassion for every individual whose mind is unfortunately developed.— Gt. Har. Vol. 3, p. 71.

CONFESSION.

The beautiful human heart, the seat and symbol of the affections, cannot safely conceal its sorrows. Open confession to some worthy person, notwithstanding the immediate pain and mortification, is often a perfect prevention of insanity.— Temple, p. 389.

CONSOLATION.

Consolation, which can save mankind, comes over the paths of knowledge.— Eth. of Conj. Love, p. 142.

COMMUNION.

You who would learn the truth should go into the most secret chamber of your own souls. The spirit of God lives there. There you should go to pray, to sing, to commune with your guardian spirits.—Gt. Har. Vol. 3, p. 44.

CHARITY.

In the steady discharge of her mission, Charity is tender, gentle, unpretending, and strong.— Gt. Har. Vol. 2, p. 107.

If charity is properly directed, and unrestrained while walking in the holy avenues of Wisdom, her deeds will unfold like heavenly violets in the garden of the Soul, and spread the fragrance of happiness wherever she treads.— Gt. Har. Vol. 2, p. 105.

CULTIVATION.

The mind is capable of growth and endless progression. It can be cultivated like a flower, until its immortal fragrance shall be sweet, and pure, and spiritual.— Gt. Har. Vol. 2, p. 131.

CONTEMPLATION.

Universal love inspires the individual with enlarged sympathies; warms the intellect into unquenchable thirstings after boundless knowledge; urges the imagination to the contemplation of interior and infinite things.— Gt. Har. Vol. 4, p. 99.

COMMUNICATIONS.

The notes of music which come through spiritual communications — from the lofty summits of heavenly inspiration — enable us to catch but imperfect glimpses of the "good time" when the earth shall ripen and blossom as the rose.— Free Thoughts on Religion, p. 123.

CALMNESS.

If you desire calmness in the midst of a storm, then study the wonders of the inner universe ; learn the laws by which it is controlled. You are yourselves universes in miniature.— Gt. Har. Vol. 3, p. 219.

CHARACTER.

Character is the way, the fashion, the manner, the expression, the fulcrum, as well as the lever, by and through which the soul announceth and declareth itself to the external world.— Penetralia, p. 399.

CONVICTIONS.

Look within for that principle which causes all effects in the external. When you find an internal conviction that you are immortal, which no sophistry can invalidate or disturb, then you have found *a treasure*, the beauty of which is greatly enhanced by spiritual manifestations.— Penetralia, p. 254.

CONFIDENCE.

Give a man confidence in himself that he hath an inward character, and he will forthwith commence the work of reform and self-purification.— Penetralia, p. 443.

CHARITY.

Charity educates and expands the perceptions, and conceptions, and all other attributes of the soul. . . . She teaches the soul to feel its individuality, to acknowledge its dependence, and cultivate the spirit of a universal relationship.— Gt. Har. Vol. 2, p. 106.

CONDEMNATION.

There is nothing that can condemn evil but goodness. The angel of the human heart looks mournfully upon the wrong deeds of the creature man. The still small voice is forever in the presence of the transgressor ; and there is no escaping its noontide and midnight injunctions.— Gt. Har. Vol. 3, p. 358.

CREEDS.

It is better to believe in the human soul, when exalted by purity of thought and harmoniousness of life and purpose, than in any creed in the wide world.— Gt. Har. Vol. 3, p. 268.

CONFIDENCE.

In order to have a true faith and confidence in the existence, wisdom, power, and love of the Supreme Being, the mind must interrogate its own depths, and watch the mysterious workings of its own properties and principles.— Gt. Har. Vol. 2, p. 374.

CONVERSATION.

Conversation is a powerful means of spirit-culture and harmony. It touches the social chords of sympathy, and inspires the spirit with new sentiments and language. It ennobles the feelings, and beautifies the general deportment.— Gt. Har. Vol. 2, p. 178.

D.

DEITY.

Deity is the source of all vitality.— Gt. Har. Vol. 1, p. 48.

DISCIPLINE.

Life is a chain of discipline. . . . There is not a chord in man's nature which some event does not strike at some time.— Inner Life, p. 107.

DESTINY.

The destiny of all men is Immortality, Happiness, and Progression.— Gt. Har. Vol. 1, p. 41.

Let us, O let us, unfold the beauties of the spirit, study its immense possessions, and improve ourselves ; and then we will know, and feel, and form just conceptions of our mission and our destiny.— Gt. Har. Vol. 1, p. 41.

DEVELOPMENT.

Properly considered, the spiritual state is the complete development and harmonization of the individual.— Gt. Har. Vol. 3, p. 310.

DEATH.

To the convinced and enlarged understanding there is no death . . . only the most important and delightful change in the mode of personal existence.— Gt. Har. Vol. 2, p. 242.

DIVINITY.

To the spiritually minded all realities are clothed in a glowing divinity ; every-day occurrences are miraculous.— Gt. Har. Vol. 3, p. 106.

When the *mind* is exercised upon the superior planes of thought, then all material forms are invested with an unusual significance,— everything has a deep and sacred meaning,— the external world is full of Divinity.— Gt. Har. Vol. 3, p. 21.

DEITY.

Man is a portion of Nature, and Nature is ever enduring, because its soul is Deity.— Inner Life, p. 421.

DEVELOPMENT.

All belief in the High and Beautiful, in the Spiritual and Supreme, in Theism and Immortality, comes into practical form only by the soul's development.— Gt. Har. Vol. 5, p. 283.

DUALITY.

In all things, throughout the realms of mind or matter, *two opposing principles rule and work the same.*— Gt. Har. Vol. 5, p. 80.

GOD IS DUAL. . . . Better than the Virgin Mary's saintly position in the ethical temple is the simple announcement that *God is as much Woman as Man*, a one-ness composed of two individual equal halves, Love and Wisdom absolute and balanced eternally.— Gt. Har. Vol. 5, p. 196.

DESTINY.

We should not forget that we live now to live again.— Gt. Har. Vol. 1, p. 40.

DEIFICATION.

I thank God that I am permitted to raise my voice against the deification of individuals, — against every species of idolatry and super-stition.— Gt. Har. Vol. 3, p. 375.

DEATH.

Death is but an *event* in our eternal life.— Gt. Har. Vol. 1, p. 159.

Death is simply a *birth* into a new and more perfect state of existence.—Gt. Har. Vol. 1, p. 159.

DISCORD.

Let no inflated mind be unjust to *the body* within which it lives and moves, for thus "Disease" is born, and those deeper discords also that shut out the holy light of eternity.— Gt. Har. Vol. 5, p. 243.

DISCUSSION.

Fear of free discussion is the strongest sceptre in the hand of error and despotism.— Harmonial Man, p. 16.

DEMONS.

What are they? Passions, appetites, and inversions. " The only begotten " is the principle of Truth.— Morning Lectures, p. 102.

DEVELOPMENT.

To man, the universe is *great, beautiful, divine,* and *magnificent;* or it is *small, chaotic,* and *unbeautiful,*— just as he is individually organized, educated, and developed. — Gt. Har. Vol. 1, p. 178.

DEITY.

In food, water, and air the Deity lives; it is through these instrumentalities that he imparts many harmonizing and spiritualizing principles to the human constitution.— Gt. Har. Vol. 1, 275.

DEATH.

Death is largely a cleansing process, and is the hope of the world, not its point of darkness.— Death and After Life, p. 96.

DEVELOPMENT.

Every thing is unfolding life and beauty, according to the law of progressive and eternal development.— Nat. Div. Rev., p. 414.

DESTINY.

Nothing lives in vain, or is left to blind destiny ; but, otherwise, every existence is indispensible to the welfare and harmony of the whole.— Answers to Questions, p. 39.

DISCORD.

What *pain,* what internal *convulsions,* what tumultuous *pulsations* of the heart do we experience when the harsh sounds of enmity and passion grate discordantly upon the spirit ! —Gt. Har. Vol. 1, p. 82.

DUTY.

Respect for your manhood or womanhood, how small soever your gifts may be, is the first of all duties.— Penetralia, p. 106.

DEATH.

Death is but the " dark hour " which, like a herald, precedes the morning sun of a higher Life; even as earthly evil, when not abused, is the dungeon-door we pass through, to reach the goal of the absolute GOOD.— Hist. and Phil. of Evil, p. 75.

DESIGN.

The beauty and harmony of ALL THINGS; the Cause, Effect, and End; the Design; the uses; the unchangeable and eternal simplicity of movements externally manifested, still which are too immense and powerful to be comprehended,— speak only the voice of eternal Power and Wisdom ! — Nat. Div. Rev., p. 111.

DIVINITY.

Divinity, in its central life, IS LOVE. In this truth you behold the source of "Salvation" to yourself and to all your neighbors in the wide world.— Stellar Key, p. 164.

DEIFICATION.

All over-statement is injustice ; the deification of persons is a "spot on the sun" of righteousness. Every exaggeration of supposed gods, every over-statement of the wisdom of spirits, is followed by a corresponding diminution of mankind.— Penetralia, p. 169.

DEPENDENCE.

We must not accustom our minds to depend too much upon the guardian spirit for direction and happiness. When we ascertain our duty and destiny, or obtain certain convictions concerning them, we should act in strict accordance with all the light we possess.— Gt. Har. Vol. 3, p. 328.

DESIRE.

Each radical human *desire* is a promissory note, drawn up and endorsed by the Eternal God, payable at the ever-solvent Bank of Ultimate Satisfaction.— Penetralia, p. 107.

DIAKKA.

Identification, at a spirit-circle, is, in the present stage of our development, almost impossible. One day your *real* friend or relative will communicate, next time the fun-loving Diakka will simulate your friend's character and do all the honors.— Diakka, p. 80.

DESTINY.

Man is designed for a career of endless Progression; to which process all evils and sufferings are incidental, conditional, temporal, and educational,— working out, when not abused, "a far more exceeding and eternal weight of glory."— Hist. and Phil. of Evil, p. 81.

DOUBT.

Doubt, which means uncertainty, is the mind's prime incentive to activity.—Heavenly Home, p. 39.

DELIVERANCE.

There are thousands of pure and loving angels looking upon us, desiring our speedy deliverance from discord and error.— Eth. of Conj. Love, p. 90.

DEVELOPMENT.

The full, perfect, and proportionate development of our own nature is the great end for which we should constantly and prayerfully strive.— Gt. Har.　Vol. 3, p. 224.

DIAKKA.

A Diakka is one who takes insane delight in playing parts, in juggling tricks, in personating opposite characters; to whom prayers and profane utterances are of equi value.— Diakka, p. 10.

DIFFERENCES.

The difference between men is more external than actual,— more in development than
in essence.— Har. Man, p. 150.

DESTINY.

Hidden deep in the unfathomable heart of
the infinite Mother is the sweet secret destiny
of every human heart.— Beyond the Valley,
p. 370.

DOUBTS.

The world is full of conflicting doubts and
mischievous theories, because men mix and
confound IDEAS with *thoughts*.— Gt. Har.
Vol. 5, p. 341.

DEMONSTRATION.

There is something deep, lovely, and pos-
sitive in that philosophy which demonstrates
to the unilluminated mind the possibility,
laws, and practicability of angelic intercourse
and manifestations.— Gt. Har. Vol. 3, p. 324.

DEEDS.

Every good deed dropped into the ocean of human life makes that ocean better. . . . A single benevolent act may eventually save a nation. . . . Act well your part — " the world will be the better for it."— Answers to Questions, p. 202.

DETAILS.

External history is founded on details, and details are despotic. They enslave your judgment, and force you from a generous faith to spiteful dogmatism. . . . Facts are appearances; and appearances are deceptive.— Gt. Har. Vol. 4, p. 26.

DOUBTS.

Minds not acquainted with the treasures of their own interior structure are easily driven ashore by "every wind of doctrine," or else into side-channels, where they encounter embarrassments and doubts innumerable.— Gt. Har. Vol. 5, p. 407.

DEITY.

In tree, in bird, in sky, in star, in your parents, in everything human, behold the love and will and wisdom of Deity.—Answers to Questions, p. 148.

DOCTRINES.

The doctrine of immortality and a belief in spiritual life existed in the world long before either the New or the Old Testament was written.— Nat. Div. Rev., p. 503.

DEVOTION.

So long as you do nothing to merit a loss of your own self-respect, and so long as your self-abnegation is occasioned by your devotion to what you esteem as the best truth, so long you are a safe and truly growing man.— Heavenly Home, p. 97.

E.

EVENTS.

Unlike the brute, man adds to his vision the spectacles of experience, and learns to probe the events of life.— Inner Life, p. 393.

ERRORS.

Errors, however beautiful and gold-enameled by time, must be extracted from the human mind by the archangel of eternal truth.— Death and After Life, p. 175.

EMANCIPATION.

Anything — person, influence, or principle — that lifts you out of your mental prison and emancipates you is worthy of your truest devotion until another and a newer teacher comes in answer to your newer necessities.— Hist. and Phil. of Evil, p. 218.

EXPERIENCE.

The riches of *experience* are strewn all over the highway of human progress.— Inner Life, p. 107.

ENLIGHTENMENT.

Enlightenment destroys mystery and complicity, and opens the door to grandeur, resting upon simplicity.— Gt. Har, Vol. 3, p. 195.

EDUCATION.

Experience is the book of life. And he is a good student who knows how to read its doctrines; and he who practically acts upon them is educated in the school of God.— Inner Life, p. 392.

ETHICS.

That system of ethics is good for nothing which comes not home to our business and bosoms; the congenial companion at once of our Instincts and our Reason; the guardian angel of our being — Inner Life, p. 33.

EXPERIENCE.

A rough experience works out much good;
for all evil, in the end, is overruled by right.
— Inner Life, p. 396.

ERROR.

Truth is always simple, whilst Error is
compound and generally incomprehensible.—
Gt. Har. Vol. 3, p. 195.

ETERNITY.

Eternity is an infinite ocean, and this life
is but a single drop of its everlasting waters.
— Gt. Har. Vol. 2, p. 365.

EXTERNALS.

Just in proportion as you grow independ-
ent of externals,— just in proportion as you
rise out of passions, appetites, unclean spirits,
and demons,— in that same proportion you enter into the kingdom of harmony.— Thoughts
Concerning Religion, p. 149.

ERROR.

Truth is simple and natural; Error is compound and artificial.— Phil. of Spec. Providences, p. 39.

EXPRESSIONS.

All things visible are expressions of an interior productive cause, which is the spiritual Essence.— Stellar Key, p. 118.

EXACTNESS.

Intellectual, or scientific, and mechanical *exactness* is the foundation and precursor of *spiritual truthfulness.*— Gt. Har. Vol. 5, p. 22.

EDUCATION.

Immortal *ideas* more than *transient* thoughts, and fixed *principles* rather than fleeting facts, should be roused in the young mind as the only foundation of scientific and moral improvement.— Hist. and Phil. of Evil, p. 132.

EVIL.

What is termed evil generally develops good.— Gt. Har. Vol. 1, p. 148.

ENEMIES.

If you walk one mile with your enemy, he will try to force you to go twain. Beware of the "first false step."— Diakka, p. 15.

ERRORS.

Abandon error as soon as you discover it in any department of your nature. Remove all stones from your grain fields. One truth is better than all the errors of Christendom. — Eth. of Conj. Love, p. 132.

EQUILIBRIUM.

To be wholly material is to be deprived of the blessings which flow from the spiritual; and to be wholly spiritual, in this sphere of existence, is to be unphilosophical and discordant.— Inner Life, p. 365.

ERROR.

Error is mortal and cannot live, and Truth is immortal and cannot die.— Nat. Div. Rev., , p. 1.

EQUALITY.

Each human soul is identical in germ. There is no *essential* difference between men. — Gt. Har.   Vol. 4, p. 48.

ENDOWMENTS.

No man or woman, educated to realize all the noble capacities of the human spirit, can consent to pass a life unworthy of innate powers and endowments.— Hist. and Phil. of Evil, p. 220.

EXISTENCE.

Our existence after death is not ghostly and ghastly, but is natural, palpable, definable, and most desirable,— a relative existence, as much in harmony with objects and substances as the present.— Memoranda, p. 232.

ENERGIES.

Spirit-principles and energies impregnate and saturate with interior life every particle, every organ, every fibre, every force, every ether, and every essence within or about the individual organization.— Temple, p. 18.

EXPRESSION.

Simplicity in expression is a partial test of truth,— and yet, some truths are so fine, so exquisitely attenuated, that to treat them with simple words seems somewhat like dressing a divine and gentle spirit in homespun sackcloth.— Answers to Questions, p. 60.

EXPERIENCES.

If it be true that John saw an angel standing in the sun, or if it be true that any man at any time ever saw a spirit, it is most reasonable to presume that *the same experience* will continue to form a part of all human history.— Answers to Questions, p. 10.

EFFECTS.

Awaken the Intellect, and set it at work, and the effect is skepticism and agitation; unfold Wisdom, and the effect is spiritual faith in things eternal.— Beyond the Valley, p. 361.

EXCESSES.

All excess is vicious. . . . Let us handle the proofs of our immortality very tenderly, for they are of all evidences the most sacred to human progress; but let no man dare degrade them by over-consumption and irreverent familiarity.— Answers to Questions, p. 88.

EVIDENCES.

The exquisitely sensitive mental condition necessary for the reception of spiritual evidences, and the general ignorance of the laws controlling such conditions, is the chief reason why so many persons have reaped from the experience far more confusion than happiness. — Temple, p. 238.

EQUALITY.

The illumination of all the faculties is equal in the Spiritual State.— Gt. Har. Vol. 3, p. 290.

EXPERIENCE.

The Law of Progress is a ready writer; its ink is life; its pen, all the human world; its volume, *Experience.*— Hist. and Phil. of Evil, p. 9.

EPITAPHS.

The grave is the sweetest sorrow,— it is wreathed in a mystic solitude, with enchantments for the heart. The kindest thought is the parent of the epitaph.—Inner Life, p. 157.

ERRORS.

Errors, like the shadows of escaping clouds, will disappear when the " Sun of Righteousness" — of wisdom, truth, and brotherly love — shall send its all-searching light and healing warmth into their midst.— Approaching Crisis, p. 150.

ETERNITY.

Whoso questions Nature aright truly reads the scriptures which teach of God and Eternity.— Death and After Life, p. 176.

ERROR.

Error is the misapprehension of Truth. Evil consists in knowingly advocating what is misapprehended. . . . Truth and goodness, on the other hand, are the sovereign principles of existence, and in their boundless flight there is unutterable freedom.— Answers to Questions, p. 151.

EVIDENCES.

Man's immortality, to be of any practical service to him, *must be felt in his religious nature*, and not merely *understood* by his intellectual faculties. . . . True evidences come through the two sources Intuition and Reflection,— through the inward sources of Wisdom.— Penetralia, p. 248.

F.

FIDELITY.

If the soul is faithful to Nature and her principles, there can and will be no limits to its health, happiness, and power to work the sublimest miracles. The faithful spirit is God-like in its every manifestation.— Gt. Har. Vol. 1, p. 295.

FABLES.

By scanning the fables of the past and comparing them with the realities of the present, we can see that what were considered miraculous and supernatural are now recognized as the "matter-of-course" triumphs of progressive science,— as things ordinary and natural to the constitution of matter and principles.— Inner Life, p. 1.

FACTS.

Facts are only things, but truths are principles.— Gt. Har. Vol. 1, p. 178.

FORCES.

Nature, through all her forces, works for the development of individualized human beings.— Phil. of Spir. Inter., p. 354.

FREEDOM.

Mind is immortal. Mind is imperial. It bears no mark of high or low, rich or poor. It heeds no bound of time or place, of rank or circumstances. It asks but freedom.— Har. Man, p. 23.

FOUNTAINS.

The immortal spirit is the fountain. The everlasting waters of this fountain are its principles of love. The final coherent manifestation of these principles, in their totality, is called wisdom.— Fountain, p. 114.

FIDELITY.

Fidelity is the integrity of your soul to itself,— obedience to the angel of God within, — to your best and highest attractions.— Penetralia, p. 82.

FACULTIES.

Like immortal jewels dropped from the divine Crown, harmoniously set in the earthen ring of the familiar microcosm, so man's faculties shine forth practically, throughout the life and lip and deeds of all the after ages.— Hist. and Phil. of Evil, p. 14.

FLOWERS.

Fix your affections upon flowers; let the *thorns* take care of themselves. Lift your eyes toward the mountains; let the *dark ravines* exist where they must. Become a seer of the good that men do; let their evils make but little impression upon your judgment.— Answers to Questions, p. 222.

FORMS.

Forms are the thoughts of Nature, as thoughts are the forms of the mind.— Nat. Div. Rev., p. 315.

FIRMNESS.

Be thou *firm* in the ways of wisdom; then the angels will kindly look down and bless you.— Temple, p. 322.

FEAR.

Ignorance married to mind begets that most helpless and wretched of psychological children, called fear.— Hist. and Phil. of Evil, p. 18.

FREEDOM.

That mind which has stricken off the shackles of mental slavery, and which, with new-born gladness, realizes the eternal dignity and birthright of individual life, is certain to sing the songs of Freedom and of boundless Reform.— Answers to Questions, p. 6.

FEAR.

Let us speak *all the truth* we have the power to behold, and fear not.— Gt. Har. Vol. 5, p. 327.

FASCINATION.

There is a resistless fascination in a person who is well-balanced and wholesome.— Eth. of Conj. Love, p. 84.

FLOWERS.

Flowers bloom o'er the death-bed of that mind which sees God's smiles behind frowning clouds and tempests.— Phil. of Spir. Inter., p. 345.

FRIENDSHIP.

What *pleasure* do we derive from the sweet, musical voice of friendship and affection, sweeping with winning tones the chords of the soul, and awakening the harmony of its ten thousand strings! — Gt. Har. Vol. 1, p. 82.

FORMATION.

The Harmonial Philosophy, . . . affirms the eternity of matter,— that there is *no crea-tion*, but FORMATION.— Inner Life, p. 52.

FULFILLMENT.

To *be more*, and to profess less, is fulfilling life's grand objects, and taking a diviner posi-tion in the universe.— Thoughts on Religion, p. 71.

FORCE.

In force you see what is rudimental; in power that which is sublime. No defeat in power; always defeat in force.— Hist. and Phil. of Evil, 203.

FREEDOM.

The mind is designed for boundless free-dom ; its aspirations are unto the beautiful, the glorious, the sublime, and unto the Great Moving Principle of the Universe.— Gt. Har. Vol. 2, p. 255.

FAITH.

Faith is the innate affirmation of the immortal spirit.— Beyond the Valley, p. 319.

FIRMNESS.

Be just and natural in your spiritual growth ; then you will be as firm as the everlasting hills.— Thoughts on Religion, p. 196.

FORMS.

When the mind elevates itself to higher thoughts and purposes, all forms and uses receive an inner and more profound signification. All life, too, receives a deeper and holier explanation.— Memoranda, p. 257.

FAITHFULNESS.

Act well the part of a spiritual being ; be faithful to what is true and good ; the future will take loving care of both itself and you. This is the heavenly rest that comes from true inspiration of ideas.— Death and After Life, p. 172.

G.

GENIUS.

Behind all beautiful robes is always hidden and neglected some divinely commissioned genius.— Gt. Har. Vol. 5, p. 240.

GENERALIZATIONS.

The developed mind flies away from the "sphere of facts, and seeks rest and refreshment among genial generalizations."— Gt. Har. Vol. 4, p. 27.

GROWTH.

All true moral growth and wisdom are the higher departments of a divine Temple, whose foundations rest upon the broad granite basis of science, and whose turrets extend far above into the tranquil realms of celestial life.— Gt. Har. Vol. 3, p. 23.

GOODNESS.

Perfect justice and boundless *goodness*, upon which the infinite Temple of the Father and Mother is constructed and inflexibly upheld, are the everlasting principles of a true, universal, and all-satisfying Religion.— Heavenly Home, p. 204.

GRATITUDE.

When the sky pours out its tears, when the tempest strikes the sea, when nature portends her elemental strifes, and the thunders leap down the wild mountains, rushing with all the wildness and power of the cataract ; then — then be calm and believing ; for when the shower is past, when the clouds pass away, when the sun shines out again over the green fields, over the green lawns and variegated meadows, then the *good of the whole is revealed*, and a million birds will join numberless flowers in a hymn of gratitude for all that is passed.— Inner Life, p. 108.

GOVERNMENT.

Self-government in the individual is possible only in that state of mind which rests upon Justice,— upon the unselfish light of eternal Love and wisdom. The same is true of a nation.— Arabula, p. 154.

GOODNESS.

Wisdom sees a central element of goodness in the soul,— an angel, sleeping enfeebled, in life's manger,— and not a fiend, not a self-conscious devil, as taught by the mistaken priesthood.— Temple, p. 357.

GOD.

Every man of reason and every woman of intuition knows that God is in the deepest Heart,— an inexhaustible fountain of Love, as well as of Wisdom,— expanding through all that illimitable structure which we call "the physical universe."— Thoughts on Religion, p. 80.

GROWTH.

Universal growth in the spiritual, and a corresponding advancement in true individual manhood and womanhood, constitute the only prevention of abounding sorrows and insanity. — Temple, p. 341.

GUIDANCE.

Be guided by *Principles*, not by spirits; by Reason, not by the high-sounding dictum, or the soft persuasions, emanating from any external source. Be yourself wholly. —Eth. of Conj. Love, p. 66.

GOD.

God is the central magnet of the universe; the spiritual world is the continuation of the natural world; and man's spirit comes out of his brain at death just as the flower comes out of the bud in the garden; it is all beautifully natural, and there is no miracle.— Thoughts on Religion, p. 196.

GOD.

God is an Eternal Magnet of concentrated goodness.— Gt. Har. Vol. 2, p. 349.

GOVERNMENT.

As a nation we need less government and more growth.— Penetralia, p. 386.

GOSPELS.

Blessed are the truly wise, for they can everywhere read the gospel of Deity.— Inner Life, p. 67.

GROWTH.

Growth is the central law of our being and the object of all exertion, as it will be the result of all experience.— Arabula, p. 400.

GRACE.

Grace in the affections lends beauty to the face and sweetness to the body. One cardinal grace is sincerity, which is the key to endur-ing and perfect confidence.—Fountain, p. 119.

GODLINESS.

To be like God let us aspire to God.— Gt. Har. Vol. 2, p. 180.

GREATNESS.

Divine greatness is reflected in all things. — Gt. Har. Vol. 2, p. 36.

GERMS.

From a germ of good and truth all things, as well as all philosophies, were and are developed.— Gt. Har. Vol. 1, p. 240.

GENTLENESS.

Love that which is lovely, and deal gently with that which has been misdirected or imperfectly developed.— Nat. Div. Rev., p. 414.

GUARDIANS.

Our guardian spirits come from a fairer and serener Home than ours. . . . They come to make us better, wiser, and happier.— Gt. Har. Vol. 3, p. 317.

H.

HARMONY.

Harmony is the guardian angel of universal Love.— Gt. Har. Vol. 2, p. 155.

HOPE.

The expanding inspirations of deathless
Hope glow potentially within the surging
soul.— Hist. and Phil. of Evil, p. 31.

HAPPINESS.

Happiness very slowly comes to one who
persists in the states of discord. Beautiful
music, the fragrance of flowers, the luxurious
melody of singing birds, and the musical
voices of many waters, come only when you
internally *deserve* them.— Death and After
Life, p. 25.

HAPPINESS.

For physical happiness obey the physical laws; for organic happiness obey the organic laws; for moral happiness obey the moral laws.— Gt. Har. Vol. 3, p. 344.

HEALTH.

Moral health depends more upon physical harmony than upon the writings of religious chieftains or upon the prayers of the so-called contrite heart.— Gt. Har. Vol. 3, p. 229.

HYPOCRISY.

A selfish man, a deceiver, a hypocrite,— a man who lives in his family like a beast and before folks like a gentleman,— has not experienced a change of heart. A swinish character always gets "lengthwise in the trough." He stretches himself at full length in the advantages of his home, and closes out the choicest friends of his wife and children.— Free Thoughts, p. 146.

HEALTH.

Health of body and mind is happiness of body and mind.— Gt. Har. Vol. 1, p. 44.

HABITS.

Man should *regulate* his life, and all his habits, by the solar laws of nature.— Gt. Har. Vol. 4, p. 166.

HARMONY.

If the individual is unfolded into Harmony with himself, he has grown into immediate connection with the spiritual World.— Gt. Har. Vol. 2, p. 156.

HOMES.

The Spirits' Home is a natural world, regulated by natural laws, covered by a natural firmament, animated by a natural Deity, populated by natural spirits and angels who were once men and women, and it is therefore *natural* that dwelling-places should diversify the landscape.— Answers to Questions, p. 64.

HUMILITY.

It would seem to be a universal law that the sweetest flowers grow in the vales of humility.— Inner Life, p. 93.

HOSPITALITY.

Great minds overlook the small, and capacious hearts make room for the discords of the undeveloped.— Answers to Questions, p. 369.

HABILIMENTS.

Unmask thyself, and wear no garb but what Nature gave. Appear as thou art,— the eternal child of an Eternal *Father!*— Gt. Har. Vol. 2, p. 70.

HAPPINESS.

Learn to be wise and gentle; and add to gentleness, love; and to love, wisdom; and wisdom, being pure, begets illumination, and illumination, happiness.— Gt. Har. Vol. 2, p. 58.

HOPE.

The hope of immortality is an evidence beyond the reach of argument.— Gt. Har. Vol. 5, p. 299.

HATRED.

The indescribable meanness of gold grabbers and gold worshippers is transcended only by the unspeakable meanness of those who hate and envy them.— Temple, p. 437.

HAPPINESS.

The secret of happiness consists in removing *unnecessary friction* in one's own pathway, and in assisting to remove it from the pathway of others.—Thoughts on Religion, p. 170.

HOME.

Happy are they who, because of their harmony and freedom of Soul, cannot *depart* from home, . . . being, in themselves, the very essence and elements of its constitution. — Gt. Har. Vol. 2, p. 195.

HAPPINESS.

Happiness is an effect, of which *goodness* is the only possible cause.— Gt. Har. Vol. 5, p. 101.

HARMONY.

Unto those who live in the kingdom of harmony all good and all truth and all the joy of righteousness shall be added.— Beyond the Valley, p. 367.

HOPE.

When the sun of Reason absorbs its far-spreading radiance and disappears behind the hills of Reflection, and a mental twilight comes on, drawing a dark curtain of doubts o'er the soul's immediate prospect,— then it is that, through the darkness and despair, gleam the innumerable stars of Hope which, like the royal orbs of light that traverse the boundless domain of immensity, are visible and beautiful only when the sun sinks behind the western hills.— Gt. Har. Vol. 5, p. 297.

HARMONIES.

The universal Harmonies of the spiritual world are based upon the principles of Love and Wisdom.— Gt. Har. Vol. 3, p. 229.

HAPPINESS.

Only those who lovingly and willingly live to benefit the world find true happiness in the bosom of Nature and God.— Arabula, p. 402.

HEREDITY.

Blessed is he who possesses the power (of Knowledge) and the will (of Spirit) to rise triumphant over his incidental discord and hereditary imperfections.— Temple, p. 331.

HARMONY.

When the individual is perfectly healthy, . . . the organization is a splendid representation of spiritual beauties, musical harmonies, and symmetrical developments.— Gt. Har. Vol. 1, p. 97.

HARMONY.

The higher and more harmonious the mind the nearer does it approach to the Divine Centre,— the inexhaustible Fountain of Love, Power, and Wisdom.— Gt. Har. Vol. 5, p. 414.

HUMANITY.

Humanity is destined to sweep onward through and through evil — through wars and through justice and peace — until the marvellous melodies of the Summer Land mingle with the sympathies and happy music of mankind.— Beyond the Valley, p. 150.

HEAVEN.

When you are truly consecrated to *a principle*, the kingdom of heaven is very near to you, and you are very near to it, and it is no longer necessary that you should hire ministers to steer you along the road to a salvation from the consequences of sin.— Arabula, p. 385.

HEALTH.

In perfect health . . . the spiritual principle is refined and attracted upward by the
Divine Mind.— Gt. Har. Vol. 1, p. 95.

HEREDITY.

The mind may, by the exercise of its own
great love-and-will powers, eliminate both
the causes and the consequences of its inherited faults, evils, and error.— Heavenly
Home, p. 275.

I.

IDEALS.

Every man in his best moments has an
Ideal self to which he aspires,— a spiritual
magnet, so to speak, drawing him onward
and upward above the crudities of his animal
nature.— Inner Life, p. 69.

IDEAS.

An idea is the *form* or organization of a conception; the latter is the soul of the former.— Gt. Har. Vol. 2, p. 257.

INFINITY.

Infinity is as many times *more infinite* than you now suppose as there are *moments* in your eternal life.— Gt. Har. - Vol. 1, p. 177.

IMPERFECTIONS.

The divine cannot flow into human structures without the former participating in the *imperfections* of the latter.— Iuner Life, p. 57.

ILLUMINATION.

If we desire reliable illumination, let us go upon the Alps of personal harmony. If we would hear the " voices of angels " understandingly, let us go upon the mounts of purification, temperance, and simplicity.— Inner Life, p. 368.

INTUITION.

The voice of Truth is heard whispering its *first* melodies in the soul's intuitions.— Inner Life, p. 67.

INSPIRATION.

It signifies the inflowing of thought,— the breathing in of sentiments.— Inner Life, p. 69.

INDIVIDUALITY.

Every spirit is developed and organized sufficiently unlike any other spirit, or substance in the universe, to maintain its individuality throughout eternal spheres.— Gt. Har. Vol. 1, p. 189.

INFLUENCES.

There is not a budding rose, not a desert flower, not an ocean gem, not a star that gleams, nor a stream that ripples by, that does not exert its own peculiar influence upon the mind.— Gt. Har. Vol. 1, p. 95.

INTUITION.

Intuition is the Soul's telegraph,— *transmitting truths from the depths of Genius to the summits of Wisdom,*—informing, as by a single flash, the internal man of that which he might otherwise be long years in learning by the external methods of investigation. . . . Woman is more endowed with "Intuition" than man.— Inner Life, p. 46.

ILLUMINATION.

The superior condition, like the diamond in the enamel, is set in the framework of individual harmony,—harmony in the broadest and highest sense. Such harmony is the foundation, the germ, and the supporter of spiritual illumination. . . . Men will become mentally exalted and spiritually minded just as fast as they subjugate the material to the spiritual; the body to the mind; the present to the future; the passions to the Reason.— Gt. Har. Vol. 3, p. 285.

INTEGRITY.

There is no power more positive to evil than absolute self-integrity, or than innate love and practice of unselfish goodness.— Temple, p. 263.

INSPIRATION.

Like everything else in this universe of progression and development, true inspiration is of various kinds and graduated by innumerable degrees, as regards quality and quantity, . . . it is the illuminating presence and influence of God in the soul.— Gt. Har. Vol. 3, p. 296.

IMMORTALITY.

It is a tremendous thought, *that a human being*, once born, *can never die!* . . . Onward lives triumphantly *the real internal man.* . . . Onward forever we go,— the embassadors of infinite uses, of eternal benefits. We should be properly born, then, as well as properly educated.— Gt. Har. Vol. 4, p. 358.

IGNORANCE.

Ignorance is a negative or passive fulcrum upon which the intellectual lever of spiritual progress acts with an almighty and universal sweep.— Hist. and Phil. of Evil, p. 75.

INDIVIDUALITY.

The material organism is designed specifically and fundamentally to perform the function of giving individuality to the spiritual elements.— Answers to Questions, p. 55.

IMPATIENCE.

The wickedest demon of our day is the imp of impatience. He attacks the nerves, and in the twinkling of an eye his victim is in a "murderous rage." He kindles a great fire in the blood; he attacks the throbbing heart, and runs over the bosom the fingers of death; then down goes his object, subject, and slave, covered with the black mantle of "sudden disease."— Temple, p. 49.

INFANCY.

It is mental infancy which believes in a fickle and wrathful God.— Fountain, p. 191.

INTUITION.

Intuition tells you that you are related to an inner universe.— Beyond the Valley, p. 389.

IGNORANCE.

The doctrine that "this life is a vale of tears,"—"a fleeting show,"—"a place originally designed to try men's souls,"— is, as I see it, the doctrine of ignorance.— Inner Life, p. 400.

INSPIRATION.

A quickening and vivification of the truth-attracting affections natural to man *is inspiration; revelation* is the appropriation and comprehension, by the truth-containing faculties, of the resultant thoughts and ideas. — Gt. Har. Vol. 5, p. 16.

INCARNATION.

The holy elements and attributes of God are incarnated in every human spirit.— Gt. Har. Vol. 2, p. 180.

IMPERISHABLENESS.

Look within thee, O man, and behold the imperishable, . . . the inmost, the harmonial, and the everlasting.— Penetralia, p. 441.

IDEAS.

Ideas are principles,— the *elements* from which the spirit-essence is obtained by vintage. Spirit is the ultimate *wine* of all elements; the child essentially, not by organization, but of the Paternal and Maternal fountain of Divine Unity — of "God," as before said, and "Mother" Nature. . . . Ideas, therefore, are the indwelling properties of spirit, — the intelligent constituents, or principles, of the one indivisible essence.— Gt. Har. Vol. 5, p. 63.

IMMORALITY.

He is immorally situated whose duty tells him one thing and his interests another.— Nat. Div. Rev., p. 685.

IMMUTABILITY.

Matter and mind are eternal; by marriage they propagate the worlds which swarm the vast infinitude.— Gt. Har. Vol. 4, p. 289.

INHERITANCE.

By inheritance, a single human spirit is an abridged edition of the entire universe. . . . Each contains, in focal concentration, the attributes of all.— Gt. Har. Vol. 5, p. 99.

IGNORANCE.

Ignorance, which has been, and still appears to be, inexorable in its influences must be destroyed by the annihilating hand of *Truth* and *Wisdom*, which are omnipotent.— Nat. Div. Rev., p. 16.

INVITATIONS.

Like the winged germs of autumnal flowers come the gentle invitations of angels. Over our thoughts they flow like the waves of music on the evening air.— Answers to Questions, p. 368.

INFORMATION.

Acquired information is the kit of tools, the musical instrument, or forwarding agent, by which the intuitive and inspired mind demonstrates its constructive truths and hidden melody.— Gt. Har. Vol. 5, p. 14.

INTEGRITY.

Constitutional integrity, as as effect of physical and mental equilibrium or thorough health, is the foundation of every known or imaginable excellence. It is the mathematically accurate basis on which may stand, eternally unchanged, *Truth's own Harmonial Temple.*— Gt. Har. Vol. 5, p. 17.

INQUIRY.

Free and unrestrained inquiry is necessary to moral and intellectual progress, and therefore should be encouraged.— Nat. Div. Rev., p. 9.

INTEGRITY.

Be true-hearted, reverent, and faithful,— full of integrity in the performance of all things; be firmly determined to develop and apply the principles of Nature to every thing, — and the highest happiness will be the inevitable consequence.— Gt. Har. Vol. 3, p. 228.

INTUITION.

Intuition is "*Pure Reason*," which does not always need for its growth the gymnastical exercises of the outward perceptive faculties. It is the inwrought *wisdom* of the eternal spirit, which ever transcends the schools, and confounds the templed doctors.— Gt. Har. Vol. 5, p. 14.

IDEALS.

Every person's Ideal is modified by the force and flow and shape of circumstances.— Free Thoughts, p. 154.

INTEGRITY.

Of all principles requiring strength and independence of character to maintain, there is none more conspicuous than the principle of integrity to one's own nature.— Har. Man, p. 151.

IMMORTALITY.

To the spiritually-minded, the idea of an individualized eternal existence is redolent with hallowed grandeur, and it gleams with gorgeous mysteries. . . . The wisdom-illumined soul goes soaring and singing of the excellence and beauty of the theme, and his conceptions are " as the beaded bubbles that sparkle on the rim of the cup of immortality, as wreaths of rainbow-spray from the pure cataracts of truth."—Gt. Har. Vol. 5, p. 281.

IGNORANCE.

Superficial high-mindedness, or the positive-
ness of ignorance and the pride of knowledge,
seal the soul to the influx of God's Spirit and
Wisdom.— Stellar Key, p. 19.

IDEALS.

The reformer must labor on, without im-
petuosity, without idleness, without hatred or
malace or revenge ; but with inextinguishable
aspirations toward an ideal development of
universal goodness and truth. The Ideal
first : then the Actual.— Gt. Har. Vol. 5,
p. 237.

INJUSTICE.

All injustice is to be first examined, then
understood, then acknowledged, then forgotten. A bad deed lives within us, or within
others, till love is kindled upon the soul's
altar, on the mount of wisdom, in whose flame
all wrong is utterly consumed.— Har. Man,
p. 159.

IMPRESSIONS.

Good communications depend upon *good* states of mind. If you would have *true* impressions, live *true* lives.— Inner Life, p. 368.

INSANITY.

Insanity is a disease of the mind. Disease means discord. Therefore any discord of the mind is insanity.— Eth. of Conj. Love, p. 43.

INNOCENCE.

Ignorance is the parent of unhealthy and unchaste imaginings. . . . Truth has nothing in its nature to cause a blush to mantle the cheek of innocence.— Gt. Har. Vol. 4, p. 64.

INVESTIGATION.

There is nothing too sacred or too exalted for the investigations of that soul whose religious emotions and moral dignity are inspired with a love of truth.— Gt. Har. Vol. 3, p. 51.

INFINITY.

When you truly approach the Infinite you sensibly become a part of it.— Thoughts on Religion, p. 67.

INVESTIGATION.

Anything is too holy for *an angry* debate, but *nothing is too sacred* for calm investigation.— Thoughts on Religion, p. 8.

INFIDELITY.

Infidelity is the willful violation of that within you which you believe to be Truth, Justice, Righteousness.— Penetralia, p. 82.

INSANITY.

Interpreted in the light of unchangeable principles, insanity is no more caused by the infestation of individualized demons than is dyspepsia caused by the sting of a fly, or epilepsy by the perpetual flow of Niagara Falls.— Temple, p. 72.

IDEAS.

Ideas, like worlds, are in the atmosphere. — Beyond the Valley, p. 379.

INTUITION.

Intuition is the central *dialectician* who inspects the substantial principles of truth itself, like an infallible *logician* at the throne of the superior animation, who predetermines the forms in which truth shall address itself to the individual mind.— Gt. Har. Vol. 5, p. 32.

J.

JUSTICE.

With the Deity, *Justice* is both means and end in the elaboration of the material and spiritual Universe.— Gt. Har. Vol. 2, p. 150.

JEALOUSY.

Jealousy poisons the soul, and casts a poisonous odor around to blight the happiness of all it reaches.— Eth. of Conj. Love, p. 61.

JUSTICE.

When distributive justice pervades the social world, then virtue and morality will bloom with an immortal beauty. The sun of righteousness will arise in the horizon of universal industry and shed its genial rays over all the fields of peace and plenty and human happiness.— Nat. Div. Rev., p. 782.

K.

KNOWLEDGE.

The knowledge that *personal life is continued beyond the grave* is worthy the exertions of the finest powers of every doubting mind.— Fountain, p. 219.

KNOWLEDGE.

The best knowledge in the world is attributable to the world's ignorance. . . . Defeat is just as truly a part of God's system as victory.— Phil. of Spir. Inter., p. 336.

KINDNESS.

The supreme law of kindness and love, which is justice, should govern man in all his relations and intercourse with his subordinates and servants in the floods and fields of existence.— Fountain, p. 50.

KNOWLEDGE.

Knowledge or *learning* is an effect of a multitude of facts and opinions consigned to the recesses of the memory, and which are based upon external Perception and Testimony. . . . *Knowledge is acquired and superficial, but wisdom is unfolded and intuitional.*— Gt. Har. Vol. 1, p. 216.

L.

LOVE.

Love is the *primary cause* of all phenomena in physical creation. Love is the Soul of the Deity.— Gt. Har. Vol. 2, p. 136.

LIGHT.

Light in its essence is Love; and Love is Life. . . . Light is the material vehicle of Divine Life.— Gt. Har. Vol. 1, p. 279.

LAW.

Every movement in universal Nature is a direct response to the imperative command of immutable Law, which is the rule of divine action eternally established by *Him* who presides over and animates an infinite creation! — Gt. Har. Vol. 2, p. 43.

LOVE.

To love wisely is to practice the religion of eternity.— Eth. of Conj. Love, p. 72.

LENIENCY.

He who is truthful and free, and everywhere carries with him a heart of love and kindness, measures man not by the length of his creed, but by the life within and its external manifestations.— Memoranda, p. 258.

LABOR.

All true Labor "is joy divine." . . . Castle and fortress are destroyed by the *labor* of the ivy, the lichen, and the wall-flower. Ignorance is overthrown by the labors of knowledge. Rock-built citadels decay beneath the incessant *action* of harmoniously rolling seasons. Vice is displaced by the labor of virtue. Life is exalted by the *action* of its varied elements.— Answers to Questions, p. 378.

LIGHT.

The Light which Truth giveth cannot be extinguished,— it is the Life of the Universe. —Phil. of Spir. Inter., p. 265.

LIFE.

Wherever you behold Life *there* you behold Love. . . . There is but *one* principle of Life in the universe. Life issues from a Deific Fountain; it sends forth countless streams; and each organization drinks according to its capacity.— Gt. Har. Vol. 4, p. 32.

LOVE.

Love can be free only when wholly emancipated from licentiousness. Love will never be pure until Wisdom waves the banner of liberty over its head. . . . Love must be disentangled from the webwork of ignorance. It must be upraised, and worshipped as the spirit of God in man.— Gt. Har. Vol. 4, p. 295.

LOYALTY.

Learn the beautiful lesson of strict loyalty to your deepest convictions.— Hist. and Phil. of Evil, p. 203.

LIFE.

Inasmuch as life is universal, death cannot mar the divine constitution of things.— Nat. Div. Rev., p. 669.

LIBERTY.

The safety of a true Harmonial Republic consists in *organic liberty*, which brings to every man his natural Rights and attractive Industry.— Har. Man, p. 20.

LOVE.

The deep, divine, vitalizing, vivifying, and immortal essence of the Soul is *Love;* the passive or *neutral* faculty is *Will;* the restraining, governing, dissecting, and harmonizing faculty is *Wisdom.*— Gt. Har. Vol. 2, p. 135.

LABOR.

Labor, righteously and persistently bestowed, is the surest self-answering prayer.— Fountain, p. 190.

LORD.

That innate power which takes hold upon infinitude, which is allied to justice and truth and virtue, and with all that is pure and noble and sublime,— that power, residing at the heart of your inmost life, is the coming Lord of all circumstances.— Temple, p. 12.

LIBERTY.

Beyond the valley of bondage to error and injustice you behold upon your mother's white bosom an immortal diamond,— sparkling with the prismatic splendor of a galaxy of suns,— and the name thereof is *Liberty!* All exertion, all life, all unrest, all discontent, all exerted energy mean inherent efforts for liberty.— Beyond the Valley, p. 321.

LIBERTY.

Accept the idea of human progress, and you rise out of the "slough of despond," and forthwith begin to enjoy the glorious liberty of the Sons of God.— Hist. and Phil. of Evil, p. 219.

M.

MUSIC.

Our mouths and lives will discourse sweet music if we will but correctly apply "experience" to them.— Inner Life, p. 403.

MISSION.

If you live righteously, doing *no* harm and *some* good wherever you can, then you are performing your mission. *There is nothing supernatural in it.*— Inner Life, p. 385.

MUSIC.

Every thing which moves and feels and thinks in the Omnipresent spirit of God is impregnated with music. What a gospel is this! — Inner Life, p. 402.

MATTER.

Matter does not itself perform the labor of thinking, but is the elastic, the plastic, and always-efficient agent to do the work of master-forces, which it has the privilege to clothe and to accompany.— Gt. Har. Vol. 5, p. 183.

MOURNING.

It is far more reasonable and appropriate to weep at the majority of marriages which occur in this world than to lament when man's immortal spirit escapes from its earthly form, to live and unfold in a higher and better country. . . . Robe yourselves with garments of light to honor the spirit's birth into a higher life.— Gt. Har. Vol. 1, p. 171.

MYSTERIES.

The progressive growth of the spirit in truth and right is more mysterious than the coming and going of terrestrial winds.—Death and After Life, p. 81.

MARRIAGE.

True Marriage is the most divine, sacred, and eternal of all relations into which the human and immortal Soul enters. . . . A *true* union, a *true* oneness of Soul, is developed by an internal affinity, by the interior and eternal Law of Association.—Gt. Har. Vol. 2, p. 193.

MIND.

The mind is designed for boundless freedom; its aspirations are unto the beautiful, the glorious, the sublime, and unto the Great Moving Principle of the Universe. . . . The mind seeks eternal things because it is itself everlasting and eternal.—Gt. Har. Vol. 2, p. 255.

MOTIVES.

Motives, when high, lift up the soul, which is thus prepared to be a better neighbor and more successful in all the genuine enterprises of present life.— Death and After Life, p. 99.

MERIT.

Downright reality and substantial merit drive out the devils of dress and display, just as a true diamond is most beautiful when set in plain black, with a fine thread of pure gold running round the edge of the ring.— Our Heavenly Home, p. 53.

MARTYRDOM.

There is an irresistible Gulf Stream of dis-tributive justice, with ebbless tide, palpitating with deific energy, *setting straight through the ocean of human life,* which compels a bene-fitted posterity to crown with glory the man who suffered martyrdom by mistaken ances-tors.— Penetralia, p. 174.

MAN.

Man is a "harp of a thousand strings," which, when properly tuned and played upon, gives forth the most sweet and delightful harmony.— Gt. Har. Vol. 2, p. 170.

MEMORY.

In the grave are entombed every error, regret, defect, resentment, and unkind remembrance. The look, the smile, the bearing, the good deed, the noble saying, are preserved in the palace of memory.— Inner Life, p. 156.

MEDITATION.

The reflective faculties, relaxing their hold upon passing events, repose serenely within the flowery solitudes of Wisdom. From the holy mountain of moral meditation — whereon there is an intuitive perception and realization of eternal principles — the matured mind calmly contemplates the world.— Hist. and Phil. of Evil, p. 49.

METHODS.

The laws of nature are *the eternal methods of Deity.*— Inner Life, p. 52.

MANNERS.

Manners are superior to ceremonies. The first flow out of the spirit; the latter from education.— Heavenly Home, p. 51.

MISSIONARIES.

The true missionary is a preacher and practitioner of fraternal love, justice, truth, liberty. . . . Fraternal love is the missionary blossom of a spiritual civilization.— Heavenly Home, p. 274.

MARRIAGE.

True marriage is predicated upon *mutual* conjugal attraction between two souls, whether "at first sight," or as the result of long acquaintance and intimate friendship.— Answers to Questions, p. 281.

MARTYRS.

Ignorance, the greatest foe of man, hath filled the world with martyrs.— Inner Life, p. 398.

MISFORTUNES.

Ignorance is man's strongest enemy; and the cause of his greatest misfortunes.— Magic Staff, p. 109.

MIND.

The mind is a world of powers which will not silently suffer the ignoring of self-imprisonment. A wonderful incorporation of individual self-conscious centres of thoughts.—Temple, p. 32.

MYTHS.

Could we but intelligently interrogate the rounded pebble at our feet, it would reveal to us events or acts in the elemental drama of this world more wonderful and sublime than all the myths of ancient days.— Inner Life, p. 15.

MUSIC.

Music, in its perfect and full expression, is a revelation of the whole system of Nature.— Heavenly Home, p. 109.

MAN.

Man is the *Dome* of the material creation, — the window through which heaven illuminates the earth.— Inner Life, p. 51.

MAGIC.

The magic mirror of the spiritual universe is illuminated with the white light shed abroad by the sun, visible in the firmament of the Summer Land.— Temple, p. 198.

MIND.

The mind is an instrument which, when it is tuned and set to a high note on the spiritual scale of music, the angels can awaken to the sweetest melody.— Gt. Har. Vol. 3, p. 316.

MIND.

Every mind is a lens, so to speak, on which the sun and earth paint new pictures.— Inner Life, p. 406.

MARRIAGE.

There is but one true marriage, namely: *the marriage of the right man with the right woman, forever.*— Memoranda, p. 248.

MYTHOLOGY.

Mythology has resulted from prior ignorance and misconception; and superstition, sectarian affection, and prejudice, have arisen out of Mythology.— Nat. Div. Rev., p. 433.

MURDER.

Murder and every other manifestation of insanity will die and be forgotten *when mankind beget harmonious children*, and establish a system of favorable circumstances for their education and development.— Eth. of Conj. Love, p. 43.

MANHOOD.

Healthy Manhood is distinguished from Youth by serenity and intelligence.— Hist. and Phil. of Evil, p. 39.

MELODY.

It imparts grand melody to be in harmony with flies and flowers. Birds and beetles are nature's own productions.— Gt. Har. Vol. 4, p. 23.

MEDITATION.

The more the soul dwells and meditates upon divine themes the more will its capacity be enlarged and its affections refined and chastened.— Gt. Har. Vol. 2, p. 373.

MYTHOLOGY.

The more aged a doctrine is shown to be, — like the mythology of hell, and evil spirits, and a devil,— the more we should question its soundness.— Gt. Har. Vol. 3, p. 142.

MORALITY.

. True morality is the living-out of *your own ideas* and sentiments of true religion.— Penetralia, p. 81.

MUSIC.

Music is a representation of divine *Order;* and *Order* is the Wisdom of the Deity.— Nat. Div. Rev., p. 737.

MISERY.

All happiness, like all misery, results from, or is the effect of, *conditions within and circumstances without.*— Answers to Questions, p. 188.

MOTIVES.

Streams of good and healthy motives will spring up to cleanse and refresh the moral world, on whose advancing tide the race will ascend to intellectual and social harmony, and to a high state of spiritual elevation.— Gt. Har. Vol. 2, p. 43.

MECHANISM.

This world is the manufactory of spirits; the store-house is the Spirit Land.— Inner Life, p. 394.

MIND.

The human mind is constituted for an eternal search after and progression in *Good*.— Fountain, p. 245.

MEDIATOR.

Man stands on the apex of the magnificent pyramid of the visible organic creation,—" a little lower than the angels." He is the pneumatic bridge over which every thing spiritual travels into this world.— Inner Life, p. 56.

N.

NOBLENESS.

Nothing noble or heroic can be achieved without labors and dangers of greater or less magnitude.— Fountain, p. 219.

NATURE.

Like a gift from God thou art,— a throb from the Deific Heart,— a pledge from the Soul of Supreme Truth.— Gt. Har. Vol. 4, p. 288.

NOBILITY.

If you wish to acquire absolute strength of body, if you desire a clear and well-balanced brain, if you want a large mind and a more noble character,— then, Breathe, Breathe, Breathe "the breath of life, and become a living soul."— Harbinger of Health, p. 80.

NOW.

We are just as much in Eternity now —
this very moment — as we ever will be. The
infinite and eternal *now* is all we have to
call our own.— Gt. Har.　Vol. 3, p. 362.

NATURE.

Nature is a book whose every sentence
proves the ascension of man from a small
point of life; the first productions of Nature
are inferior to her every subsequent unfolding.— Penetralia, p. 43.

NOBILITY.

You should be distinguished from the
world's inhabitants,— by your nobility; by
your happiness; by your superior offspring;
by your high intelligence, and eloquence, and
psychological power,— by *all*, in a word,
which distinguishes the kingdom of heaven
from the discords of earth.— Gt. Har.　Vol. 3,
p. 104.

NOURISHMENT. ·

Vital magnetism and electricity are the divine elements of spiritual (not moral) nourishment, and are the mediums through which the spirit acts upon the body.— Gt. Har. Vol. 1, p. 145.

NOBLENESS.

A man must not only *know* that it is wrong to do certain things (because of the logical consequences and suffering which will follow to himself) but he must also *feel* that he is *too noble, too just, too regardful of the interests and development of kindred,* neighbor, and the world, to allow himself ever to sin against light and knowledge.— Gt. Har. Vol. 4, p. 177.

O.

ORDER.

Order and *Form*, and *Love* and *Wisdom*, are indicated in each created object, from the lowest to the highest.— Gt. Har. Vol. 2, p. 36.

OPPORTUNITIES.

With pure physical development come "golden opportunities" to be pure, and loving, and wise, and progressive in all things.— Answers to Questions, p. 212.

OPPRESSIONS.

It is culpable moral weakness of individual will — yea, it is nothing less than a wicked rejection of the Divine goodness — to drop and "give up" under the oppressions of misfortune.— Temple, p. 326.

OPINIONS.

Truthful opinions never impeach the plans of divine efforts ; neither do they afflict human souls with dismal ideas of the vast beyond.—Penetralia, p. 96.

OBEDIENCE.

The will-power of an angel is always exercised through the diamond avenues of wisdom. A wise will is very powerful.   The passions of the soul must live in eternal obedience to this indwelling wisdom attribute.—Gt. Har. Vol. 3, p. 219.

ORGANIZATION.

Man is an organization not composed of a mutual agreement of parts through the indefinite workings of an inpetuous Nature, but is rather the perfect form, the highest image, the designed organization of the divine Mind that pervades immensity.—Nat. Div. Rev., p. 351.

OMNIPRESENCE.

The divine essence is everywhere and in all things.— Gt. Har. Vol. 1, p. 263.

ORGANIZATION.

God must be himself *organized* before he can breathe forth *organization.*— Gt. Har. Vol. 1, p. 48.

OBSERVATION.

Look into the laws of life from a purely honest observation of its principles and purposes, and thus harmonize with its constitutional needs and eternal ends.— Fountain, p. 245.

OPPOSITION.

The only hope for the amelioration of the world is free thought and unrestricted inquiry. Anything which opposes or tends to obstruct this sublime and lofty principle is wrong.— Nat. Div. Rev., p. 5.

P.

PURITY.

To be pure, something besides soap and hot water is required. It is downright hard work in the character. Something besides very severe labor is also needed. It is cheerfulness of spirit and good physical habits.— Eth. of Conj. Love, p. 85.

PRAYER.

The only *prayer* I would recommend is a practically righteous life. . . . Harmonial Culture not only brings *out* that which is intrinsically constitutional, *but increases the interior power of attraction*, whereby the soul obtains the pabulum of life, and grows exceedingly — on and on, henceforth and forever.— Gt. Har. Vol. 4, p. 57.

PRAYER.

A profoundly grateful and loving heart is slow in verbal prayer and exquisitely delicate in professions.— Heavenly Home, p. 51.

PERFECTNESS.

Be instructed by the Past, and by all it has brought you. Be thankful for the Present, and for all its blessings. Be hopeful for the Future, and for all it promises to bring you. — Penetralia, p. 112.

PURPOSES.

A high, pure Purpose is possible only to *spirit*. Ambition is earthly; aspiration is spiritual. . . . Pure Purpose brings the inmost spirit into harmony with pure Truth, which is eternal. There is no failure, no defeat, no killing disappointment in the mind that is exclusively moved by a high Purpose in its external relations to mankind.— Phil. of Spir. Inter., p. 353.

PHILOSOPHERS.

Only those who search for and impart the "truth" with a harmonial love to gain the Alpine summits of "wisdom," and who labor with the unselfish aspiration to advance mankind in virtue and happiness, are worthy of the honorable title of Philosopher.— Gt. Har. Vol. 5, p. 270.

PRINCIPLES.

Truth, Love, Justice, Beauty, Liberty, Growth,— these are principles, and also the fruition of principles, which would overcome all evil, and fill the world with brotherhood, joy, peace, happiness.— Beyond the Valley, p. 257.

Great thoughts, true feelings, high truths, innate ideas, immortal principles,— these come, and these abide; they multiply and exalt all existences, and they carry us all in their bosoms, or take us by the hand, and go on forever.— Beyond the Valley, p. 58.

PHENOMENA.

The Cause of phenomena is self-intelligent, self-loving, self-rewarded, absolute, unchangeable.— Gt. Har. Vol. 5, p. 85.

PROGRESSION.

Ignorance is the diabolical monster of the human mind, and selfishness is the " roaring lion " that goes up and down the earth, seeking whom it may "devour." Progression is the angel of our deliverance.— Harbinger of Health, p. 420.

PLAYFULNESS.

The human face is provided with thousands of nerves and fibres naturally responsive to playfulness, wit, and feelings of mirthfulness, while there are exceedingly few provisions made by Providence for expressing grief, melancholy, and other bilious affections. The good and pure, in all worlds and spheres, are gay and playful.— Temple, p. 443.

POWER.

One profound student of nature will put to flight ten thousand priests whose only strength consists in their ecclesiastical organizations, and in the superstitious ignorance of their devotees.— Gt. Har. Vol. 3, p. 16.

PRAYER.

True prayer, oral or silent, is born of the bosom, not of the brain.— Fountain, p. 180.

True prayer is the glowing and graceful expression of the virgin imagination, warmed and fed by spiritual passion and devout meditation.— Fountain, p. 185.

Prayer is sometimes a key by which the golden door of infinite opportunities may be unlocked ; and, sometimes, prayer calls to our immediate aid those wise and strong guardians who daily live in harmony with the eternal currents of affection.— Fountain, p. 220.

PROGRESSION.

The *Soul* knows no retrogression, neither maturity. It is destined for eternal progression, and for the unbroken enjoyment of an immortal youth.— Gt. Har. Vol. 3, p. 65.

POWER.

When the spirits' power rises up from its inmost,— when it expands above force and war, both private and public,— it sees itself to be "a conqueror" in the midst of its material surroundings.— Arabula, p. 384.

POPULARITY.

If men loved Truth more than the honey-comb of Popularity,— worshipped Principle more than the gold which devotion to fashionable "vital Piety" brings them,— then, indeed, would come the good time — the Platonic Era — when Truth and Peace, Law and Liberty, *shall reign supreme.*— Inner Life, p. 61.

POWER.

If we would learn of the dignity and power of humanity, we must study "The Individual."—Inner Life, p. 42.

PERFECTION.

The more perfect your intuition of principles the nearer you are to the heart and soul of things.— Heavenly Home, p. 147.

PHILOSOPHY.

The Harmonial Philosophy . . . is a revelation of the Natural, Spiritual, and Celestial departments of God's Universal Temple.— Gt. Har. Vol. 2, p. 104.

PRAYER.

True spirit-prayer, like the glory of morning dew, ascends noiselessly. The answer? *that* comes, welcome as the fall of rain, when the soul most needs nutrition.— Penetralia, p. 78.

PASSIONS.

Passionate emotions are fleeting. They are heaven's lightning flash. . . . As the flash of lightning is to the ever-shining sun, so is the fire of passion to the serene love of the spirit.— Beyond the Valley, p. 378.

PREJUDICES.

Men should not cherish prejudices against each other, so long as the sun shines to bless the earth and all men, and while the laws of Nature are unchangeable and ever impartial in their displays.— Nat. Div. Rev., p. 718.

PURIFICATION.

The calm, pure heavens are peopled with hosts of strong powers whose great sympathetic hearts beat, through all the intervening space, responsive to our every soul-born prayer for purification and righteousness. . . Every such prayer is some day answered.— Magic Staff, p. 135.

PHYSICIANS.

Nature, intuition, and circumstances are ever the best physicians.— Gt. Har. Vol. 1, p. 272.

PURPOSES.

Every mind intuitively recognizes the eternal value of pure purposes.—Death and After Life, p. 82.

PREJUDICES.

Unless we can cast off the prejudices of the man and become as children, docile and unperverted, we need never hope to enter the temple of philosophy.— Stellar Key, p. 92.

PRINCIPLES.

The word of God is composed of Love, Justice, Truth, Wisdom, and Liberty. *Principles*, wherever you find them, whether in religion or out of it, are infallible and imperishable *words of God.*— Thoughts on Religion, p. 183.

PRAYERS.

The best prayers are those which tend to the overcoming evil with good.— Gt. Har. Vol. 5, p. 379.

PERSONALITIES.

The inability to rise superior to personalities is one of the most deplorable weaknesses of our undevelopment.— Beyond the Valley, p. 394.

PUNISHMENTS.

Anything that produces discord in the physical, or social, or moral systems of our being will cause us to suffer a physical, social, or moral punishment.— Phil. of Spec. Providences, p. 68.

PERFECTION.

The mind must be *refined and perfected*, and when this is properly accomplished the social world will be correspondingly elevated, and thus be advanced to honor, goodness, and *Universal Peace.*— Nat. Div. Rev., p. 677.

PREDISPOSITION.

Every human soul has an intrinsic predisposition to goodness, to harmony, and to spiritual illumination.—Gt. Har. Vol. 1, p. 209.

PURITY.

He is spiritually-minded who considers absolute purity of heart and life to be the richest of human possession.— Penetralia, p. 105.

PEACE.

When you attain to "inward peace" you are born again. Then you can live a spontaneous, easy, free, orderly, happy life.— Free Thoughts, p. 149.

PROOFS.

There is an abundance of proof that the dwellers of the other life are in daily communication with minds of persons who yet inhabit the temple of clay.— Inner Life, p. 312.

PRINCIPLES.

Principles are everywhere operative *intelligences.*— Gt. Har. Vol. 5, p. 61.

POWER.

Use informs of Utility; *Justice* informs of Right; and *Power* executes their united *Designs.*— Gt. Har. Vol. 2, p. 151.

PEACE.

He who can carry about, in the unseen chambers of his heart, a disposition to make peace on earth and good will toward man is already in the kingdom of peace.— Gt. Har. Vol. 3, p. 360.

PROPHECIES.

Human efforts toward a true knowledge of life and its laws are in reality just so many prophecies of the discoveries of *truth*, which will ultimately triumph, and crown humanity, and finally save the world.— Temple, p. 57.

POWER.

Power, which is always from spirit, is never conquered.— Hist. and Phil. of Evil, p. 200.

PLANETS.

A planet is one of Nature's significant beads on the endless rosary, which consists of countless decades of orbs.— Answers to Questions, p. 27.

PHILOSOPHY.

Harmonial Philosophy teaches that self-possession — true self-ownership — is one of the paths leading to the *shortest* road to the kingdom of heaven.— Free Thoughts, p. 168.

PUNISHMENT.

It is philosophically impossible for punishment to be interminable. The endless duration of punishment would utterly destroy the purposes of punishment.— Answers to Questions, p. 209.

PRINCIPLES.

Principles are both omnipresent and impersonal.— Stellar Key, p. 157.

PREJUDICE.

All prejudice is bigotry, and thoughtless repudiation is foolishness.— Gt. Har. Vol. 5, p. 220.

PERFECTION.

Perfection and truthfulness of mind are the secret intentions of Nature.— Eth. of Conj. Love, p. 132.

PROGRESSION.

Progression is the path of deliverance, and blessed is he who walketh in it.— Answers to Questions, p. 185.

PERCEPTION.

The true preacher can see "sermons in stones." The good man sees "good in everything."— Inner Life, p. 393.

POWER.

Weakness is mortal, a disease ; power is immortal, being perfect health.— Beyond the Valley, p. 387.

PROGRESS.

Progress is a law of Nature. To resist the perpetual tendencies of this law is to resist the sublime workings of the universe.— Gt. Har. Vol. 1, p. 213.

PURITY.

Conceptions of *purity* and *refinement* are enlarged in proportion to the knowledge one possesses of what is *impure* and *unrefined.*— Nat. Div. Rev., p. 200.

PIETY.

True piety is a consciousness and confession of the sentiment of religion ; true morality is the intentional application of that sentiment to the affairs of life.— Gt. Har. Vol. 5, p. 209.

PRODUCTION.

Spirit will produce spirit as a flower will produce a flower.— Gt. Har. Vol. 2, p. 246.

PURSUITS.

It is wrong to devote the present life, *which is but the beginning of existence*, to insignificant and inglorious pursuits.— Gt. Har. Vol. 1, p. 434.

PERSONALITIES.

Man is the being, above all other personalities, to whom the heavenly Father turns in order to be progressively comprehended.— Gt. Har. Vol. 3, p. 141.

Q.

QUALITIES.

It is not the quantity but the *quality* of truth which makes us free.—Gt. Har. Vol. 1, p. 177.

QUIETUDE.

You can hear the voice of intuition only when you are tranquil.— Beyond the Valley, p. 365.

QUARRELS.

Local quarrels and conflicts are blemishes that affect society as ulcers affect the diseased body.—Nat. Div. Rev., p. 695.

QUERY.

When will our brave-hearted and inspired favorites ascend to the heights of infallible Reason in matters of righteousness and eternity?—Gt. Har. Vol. 5, p. 117.

QUIETNESS.

Quietness of mind is essential to interior light.— Gt. Har. Vol. 1, p. 210.

QUANTITY.

All souls begin with identical qualities, but *not* with identical quantities, of the life principles.— Gt. Har. Vol. 4, p. 50.

QUALITIES.

By quality and by quantity men are less or more in contact with the divine principles that regulate the spiritual universe.— Hist. and Phil. of Evil, p. 173.

R.

REASON.

Reason is the exponent of truth to the intellect ; even as intuition is truth's exponent to the affections.— Fountain, p. 231.

RIGHTEOUSNESS.

All truthful-mindedness is beautiful righteousness.— Gt. Har. Vol. 5, p. 275.

REVEALMENT.

The height, length, breadth, and depth of true religion are revealed and fulfilled in the union of man with the love, justice, power, and beauty of Omniscient goodness.— Arabula, p. 101.

REASON.

We behold the temple of the Infinite as one great system of unity and truth. And *reason*, not insanity, is the medium whereby we first comprehend, and then adore.— Inner Life, p. 391.

Reason is the mirror which, when untarnished by ignorance or undeformed by error, reflects the form and likeness of truth, naturally as the placid lake images forth the firmament.— Inner Life, p. 45.

REFINEMENT.

Strict adherence to rules of physical and mental discipline will always refine the feelings and elevate the mind.—Gt. Har. Vol. 1, p. 210.

RETARDATION.

Every pure and innate quality of the human soul is arrested in its growth, because society smiles not on its tenderness, nourishes not its roots, and assists not, by superior circumstances, its growth.— Nat. Div. Rev., p. 688.

REALITIES.

Motion, Life, Sensation, and Intelligence are elements as substantially real as Fire, Heat, Light, and Electricity. Mind is as much a substance as matter, only not so far down in the scale. . . . The law of mind and the law of matter is *one;* and souls and stars are moved and regulated by the same great general principle.— Gt. Har. Vol. 4, p. 279.

REVELATION.

Nature, reason, and *intuition* are the only infallible mediums of revelation,— the only *church, creed,* and *religion natural* to the mind of man.— Inner Life, p. 46.

REFORM.

Reform is kindred with sunlight, kindred with trees, with the flow of ocean, and the tide of time; and will grow naturally, as flowers come out of the ground, and as mountains rise out of the sea.—Gt. Har. Vol. 4, p. 24.

RELIGION.

The only true Religion is that which *embraces* the *universe*, reveals perfect *justice*, breathes boundless *goodness*, fills the reason with *light*, the affections with love, the sorrowing with *consolation*, the down-trodden with *courage*, and the despairing with the golden beams of eternal *hope.*—Heavenly Home, p. 205.

REFINEMENT.

All matter is perpetually on the way to spiritual association.— Gt. Har. Vol. 5, p. 184.

RECEPTIVITY.

Those immutable laws which govern the pulsations of divine vitality through the universe are so minute and righteous that the tiny flower and revolving orb alike receive life, direction, and protection according to their respective capacities and requirements. — Gt. Har. Vol. 1, p. 282.

REASON.

Have a good and benevolent reason for everything you do. Never act from a narrow, selfish impulse. Be loving and tender-hearted. . . . Never do wrong. For there are thousands of pure and loving angels looking upon us, desiring our speedy deliverance from discord and error.— Gt. Har. Vol. 3, p. 230.

RESISTANCE.

To resist the law of eternal Growth is to resist the plainest law of the universe.— Inner Life, p. 41.

RELIGION.

To willing minds the Infinite always speaks. Boundless Justice is the highest manifestation of true religion.— Hist. and Phil. of Evil, p. 93.

REQUIREMENTS.

All things receive the Spirit of God, and bathe in it, and express it in the external in exact proportion to their capacity and absolute requirements.—Gt. Har.   Vol. 3, p. 303.

REGENERATION.

" Regeneration " is a perpetual phenomenon of existence ; the result of no miraculous "change of heart," — a perennial growth in Love and Wisdom.— Hist. and Phil. of Evil, p. 92.

RELIGION.

True religion is *justice*, and *joy*, and *peace*, and *beauty.*— Approaching Crisis, p. 106.

REASON.

As Reason exalts man above, so the lack of it degrades him beneath, the animal consciousness.— Temple, p. 10.

REFORM.

The fire of dispassionate Reason will purify the hell of all past deeds. . . . Every soul is required to place some fuel under the distilling crucible. . . . Bring fuel to the fire of reform, therefore, and work to burn up your own evils. Set your alcohol on fire. Destroy all your noxious weeds of vice. Let the furnace of private redemption burn hotter and hotter until every personal discord is consumed. Fix your whole heart firmly upon what your higher faculties admire, and do their bidding.— Harbinger of Health, p. 118.

RELIGION.

In the *harmonial age, true religion is universal justice.* Everything will be attuned to the laws of equity and reciprocation.— Hist. and Phil. of Evil, p. 86.

REASON.

If there was ever a flower from the soil of heaven planted in the garden of the human soul, blooming with an ever-increasing beauty and with an eternal fragrance, it is *Reason.*— Thoughts on Religion, p. 79.

RESPONSIBILITY.

In the honest pursuit of truth each mind must employ its own immortal reason, arrive conscientiously and thoughtfully at its own conclusions, and be prepared not only to "give a reason for the hope within," but also to accept that regal responsibility which is inseparable from personality and conduct.— Temple, p. 229.

RELIGION.

Justice and truth generate happiness, the native religion of the soul.— Gt. Har. Vol. 2, p. 67.

REASON.

Reason is the full-blown flower of the spirit; its fragrance is Love and knowledge.— Penetralia, p. 240.

REFORM.

The Principle of Love is the great lever of reformation. Fear is certain to subject and paralyze the soul, but Love draws the soul above.— Gt. Har. Vol. 3, p. 355.

RESPONSIBILITY.

The effect of too much reliance upon the invisible for aid is to beget weak-mindedness and unfitness for any great work; no man can accomplish much who doubts his personal capabilities and shirks individual responsibility.— Penetralia, p. 77.

REFORM.

Thanks to the Supreme Power of the universe, the law of reform works unchangeably onward.— Thoughts on Religion, p. 7.

REASON.

Reason, on the wings of faith and justice, is a bird of paradise. Its flight is outward, onward, upward.— Thoughts on Religion, p. 21.

RITUALS.

A religion of forms, of ceremonies, of rituals, is not the religion of manhood. Men need a religion which, when defined, means Universal Justice.— Penetralia, p. 406.

REFORMATION.

Do we yearn for love, let us be loving; do we yearn for reformation, let us be reformed; do we yearn to free mankind from discord and wrong, let us be free.— Har. Man, p. 151.

RESPONSIBILITY.

The human individual's responsibility is commensurate with, or in proportion to, the mind's power to conceive of justice and freedom.— Answers to questions, p. 206.

REALIZATION.

Whether your parentage be Caucasian or African, Mongolian or Indian, Celtic or Teutonic, it is all the same. Nature will do her work, and you will experience at last a complete realization of her original Ideas.— Penetralia, p. 422.

REPENTANCE.

Repentance unto life is a resolution taken in your wisdom faculties, renouncing a personal evil habit before the whole angel-world, whose aid you invoke,— a resolution carried out, practically, in every subsequent act of your life.— Answers to Questions, p. 153.

REPUTATION.

Reputation is but a brush-heap at best. A few flashes of fire from falsehood's forked tongue would destroy it root and branch.— Magic Staff, p. 526.

S.

SPEECH.

The speech of spirits drops upon the internal tympanum like music over the sea. The words are distinct as bugle notes, but they affect the mind as childhood's kisses do the lips, leaving a sweet presence and benefaction behind them. . . . The voice of a spirit is like the spirit of truth,— most eloquent when manifested in deeds,— for thus the higher intelligences communicate their thoughts to those beneath them.— Answers to Questions, p. 72.

SPIRIT.

Spirit is an indissoluble *unity* of the finest particles of matter.— Gt. Har. Vol. 2, p. 248.

STANDARD.

Self is the eternal standard of consciousness,— the portal through which the soul looks into the far off.— Inner Life, p. 411.

SOUL.

The soul knows no retrogression ; neither maturity. It is destined for eternal progression,— for the unbroken enjoyment of an immortal youth.— Inner Life, p. 411.

SEPULCHRES.

The true Spiritualist sees that there is no sepulchre, no tomb ; . . . that death is nothing but a gentle " defeat " which excludes the cypress and includes the laurel.— Phil. of Spir. Inter., p. 345.

STANDARD.

Eternal *truth*, as it is revealed through the beautiful mediums of *love* and Justice, is the only everlasting standard.— Fountain, p. 231.

SEQUENCES.

We make (or have made by the confluence of external circumstances for us) our heaven and our hell as we journey forward; they come not as arbitrary rewards and punishments, but as inevitable *sequences* to right and wrong doing.— Penetralia, p. 224.

SPHERES.

As a tree spreadeth its branches over the weary traveller, and delighteth his sense with sweet perfume, even while he smiteth it to obtain its fruit, so do the angelic spheres — the spirit-worlds — spread themselves over earth's inhabitants, yielding them, in the still hours of life's repose, joy and holy inspiration. — Phil. of Spir. Inter., p. 265.

SUPREMACY.

A natural intuition of religious truth gives all a love of moral supremacy.— Gt. Har. Vol. 5, p. 161.

SALVATION.

We must work out "our own salvation" from the causes of unhappiness. The angels will help us just in proportion as we help ourselves.— Harbinger of Health, p. 420.

SPIRIT.

The spirit, in consequence of its outer organization, can never be lost or dissipated in any of the great cycles of the ever-changing universe.— Gt. Har. Vol. 5, p. 407.

The spirit itself is inmost and is intimately allied to the perfect and supreme. It could not be created; it could not be destroyed. It never had a miraculous beginning; it will never experience a miraculous end.— Gt. Har. Vol. 5, p. 401.

SPIRIT.

The spirit is *the wine* procured from the vintage of the universe. It is obtained from the ultimate ethers of all elements combined. — Gt. Har. Vol. 5, p. 63.

STRENGTH.

It is sublime strength and wisdom to allow the principle, "overcome evil with good," to flow up from within and over all one's relations to his fellowmen. . . . . All principles are innate, and will grow powerful in due season.— Gt. Har. Vol. 5, p. 93.

SPLENDOR.

A silent splendor floats down from the noon-day sun and illuminates the hills. Star-beams come down from on high and play amid the lilies of the valley. There is a glow and a loveliness — a poem and a song — upon, and flowing from, every thing that lives. — Inner Life, p. 13.

SPIRITUALIZATION.

The spiritual body is "matter" spiritual-ized, as the flower is the earth refined.— Inner Life, p. 55.

SORROWS.

Just above a sharp thorn the bud bursts open, and a flower unfolds. So every sorrow embosoms a joy,— every grief is accompanied by some beneficent provision to mitigate its intensity, and secure a good result.— Approaching Crisis, p. 150.

SLEEP.

It is the Soul and *not* the body which experiences exhaustion and requires sleep.— Gt. Har. Vol. 1, p. 151.

Sleep is only a mode by which the fatigued soul *partially* withdraws itself from the physical structure, and gathers inwardly for the purpose of self-recuperation.— Gt. Har. Vol. 1, p. 151.

SUBJECTIVITY.

If the mind would grow and expand from its own roots and vitality, its possessor must cultivate subjectivity of feeling and thinking. — Beyond the Valley, p. 318.

SOURCES.

There are but four general sources of thought and knowledge, namely,— the life-springs of the soul; the suggestions of external nature; the well-springs of humanity; and the exhaustless fountains of the spiritual universe.— Gt. Har. Vol. 3, p. 303.

SUBLIMITY.

How glorious and exalting to experience, in common with the manifold creations of nature, the sublime presence of the Great Spirit; how elevating to feel our souls begemmed and constantly spiritualized by the mellow, glowing light of numberless firmaments ! — Gt. Har. Vol. 1, p. 280.

SYMPATHY.

It is highly essential to our happiness and development that we allow our souls to grow into the religion of a universal sympathy.— Gt. Har. Vol. 3, p. 109.

SIN.

Sin, in the common acceptation of that term, does not really exist; but what is called sin is merely a *misdirection* of man's physical and spiritual powers, which generates unhappy consequences.—Nat. Div. Rev., p. 521.

SPIRITUALIZATION.

Spiritualization is the high inflowing flood-tide of the Divine life unto humanity; but "materialization" is the subsidence,— the backward and downward drift of the sea; and, lo! the shores thereof will be strewn with multitudinous wrecks,— doubters, agnostics, cynics, hermits, haters, heathen.— Beyond the Valley, p. 330.

SPIRIT.

The human spirit is the *focal organism* of Nature.— Inner Life, p. 54.

SCIENCE.

Science is a sure safe-guard against superstition.— Fountain, p. 231.

SECTARIANISM.

It is with you and your convictions to decide whether a *sectarian bondage* shall oppress the free-born mind, or whether *knowledge* and *universal happiness* shall bless the earth.— Nat. Div. Rev., p. 707.

SINCERITY.

A *True* word, although sown in weedy soil, will eventually be fruitful of its own seed; even so will a true life, if lived in downright sincerity, overcome disease and all hardships, even old death itself.— Beyond the Valley, p. 167.

SUNDAY.

It is right to live every day as correctly as on Sunday.— Gt. Har. Vol. 2, p. 338.

SILENCE.

True silence is the handmaid of meditation; she is a good and faithful friend to him who prays in secret.— Penetralia, p. 108.

SIN.

Sin is a name for excess,— a mark missed by man in his development; a ditch into which, when with ignorance or passion blind, we stumble for a season.— Penetralia, p. 43.

STRENGTH.

Pure spirit is above the reach of temptation. Moral strength to overcome or to resist evil is the promise of the future angel. It is, in fact, the *basis* on which the angel-character is finally erected.— Thoughts on Religion, p. 210.

SUPERSTITION.

The changing and inclement skies of super-stition entail distress and wretchedness upon human nature.— Fountain, p. 240.

SELFISHNESS.

Live selfishly for yourself and you will sit down at the end of life dissatisfied with human existence.— Phil. of Spir. Inter., p. 360.

SIGHT. ·

The physical eye can only see physical things, while the spiritual eye can behold both spiritual and physical things.— Stellar Key, p. 135.

SPIRIT.

The spirit will progress eternally. . . . Let us, then, live justly, truly, and purely; because by so doing our position will be com-manding and glorious in those numberless spheres where the spirit will reside.— Gt. Har. Vol. 2, p. 254.

SPLENDORS.

Dull minds sleep behind dull senses; but star-eyed persons possess minds shining full of heavenly splendors.— Stellar Key, p. 19.

SUFFERINGS.

Sufferings are blessings,— the evidences of Nature's justice, the careful baptism of deific love eternal.— Gt. Har. Vol. 4, p. 383.

SUBLIMITY.

This great natural universe in all its sublimity is nothing when compared with the essential properties and immortal capacities of man's spirit.— Hist. and Phil. of ·Evil, p. 217.

SELFISHNESS.

Do good from a selfish motive, and you will find a chemical poison at the very heart, which will leave your nature as poor as a miser is with his full coffers.— Death and After Life, p. 170.

SPIRITUALISM.

Spiritualism is useful as a *living demonstration* of a future existence. It abundantly proves this; but nothing else with certainty. — Magic Staff, p. 544.

SINNERS.

The sinner deserves the love and blessing of God ineffably more than the self-sustaining and well-developed; for the wise and happy need not a physician, but those only who are sick and unfortunate.— Penetralia, p. 73.

SPONTANEITY.

All *true inspiration* must be spontaneous; it must spring from the deep foundations of Nature, and seek an expression through the human soul and tongue, as the ten thousand rivulets, starting from the pregnant side of stupendous mountains, converge and mingle in the distant valley, and form the mighty ocean.— Phil. of Spir. Inter., p. 247.

SHEPHERDS.

The pure eternal Truth is man's only true shepherd. It is the diamond jewel which only God's life can make palpable to the deepest intuitions.— Beyond the Valley, p. 327.

SCENES.

I behold the spiritual sphere as containing all the beauties of the natural sphere combined and perfected. . . . Every earth is of itself an index and an introduction to the beauty and grandeur that are existing in the Second Sphere. . . . The extended surface of this Sphere, I perceive, presents regular and gentle undulations, which render the whole diversified and exceedingly inviting. Very extensive plains are presented, which are clothed with great fertility, and with innumerable varieties of forms such as deck the bosom of the earth when all things are favorable to a thrifty production.— Nat. Div. Rev., p. 653.

SKEPTICISM.

Knowledge is a constitutional *skeptic ;* Wisdom is a *believer ;* Love is a *worshipper.*—Gt. Har. Vol. 4, p. 34.

SECRETS.

You will find the scientific secrets of immortality concealed behind the underworking laws of Nature.— Gt. Har. Vol. 5, p. 384.

SPIRITUALIZATION.

That mind is most expanded and spiritualized in his thoughts and feelings who sees "God in every thing."— Answers to Questions, p. 181.

SOCIETIES.

Societies in the Second Sphere are very much to be admired, because of the perfect harmony which pervades them, and the perfect melody and concert of rudimental and perfected knowledge which they manifest.— Nat. Div. Rev., p. 650.

SELFISHNESS.

We must die to selfishness. We must forget self on the lower plane of being if we
would be happy.— Gt. Har. Vol. 3, p. 360.

SOCIETY.

Societary Harmony is an effect of Individual Harmony. Individual Harmony is an
effect of spirit growth in Love, Wisdom, and
Liberty.— Beyond the Valley, p. 400.

SCRIPTURES.

There are no scriptures more plain, more
sacred, more infallible, than the laws of life,
of health, and of a progressive experience.—
Inner Life, p. 401.

SYMPATHY.

Sympathy is compounded of healing love,
mercy, and benevolence; while false charity
is a popular mixture containing equal parts
of impulsive pity, heartless duty, and cold
contempt.— Temple, p. 412.

STRIFE.

The " Heavenly Kingdom " comes in every man's soul when he outgrows strife, selfishness, and passion, and steps upon the high table-land of peace, charity, and *Wisdom.*— Answers to Questions, p. 170.

SUPERSTITION.

Knowledge leads us progressively to the summits of immensity,— to the mounts of truth. Ignorance leads into the vales of superstition,— into the deepest pandemonium of doubt and gloom.— Inner Life, p. 42.

SOCIETIES.

It is pleasing to behold heavenly societies. I see them at this moment existing in the most perfect degree of brotherly love, and joined inseparably together by constant ascending and descending affections.— Nat. Div. Rev., p. 652.

SABBATH.

He is the worst Sabbath-breaker who cannot give some portion of every day to communion with the interior and spiritual.—Temple, p. 434.

SOMNAMBULISM.

Somnambulism is the first demonstration of the independence of the soul. It is clairvoyance undeveloped.— Gt. Har. Vol. 3, p. 241.

SUPERNATURALISM.

Human nature is not supernatural, but continues to be human,— outgrowing its errors either slowly or rapidly, in keeping with motives and temperaments.—Death and After Life, p. 61.

SPHERES.

The finest particles of all things, not absorbed by this world, go to form a spiritual globe. Like a zone on the inside of the vast Milky-Way is unfolded the Second Sphere. — Penetralia, p. 255.

T.

TRUTH.

Truth is one vast Mountain, lifting its head with exalted dignity. It stands unmoved, and will not bow to the caprices of man; yet man will progress until he reaches its very heights. — Nat. Div. Rev., p. 19.

TRANQUILITY.

The twilight hour is the period for tranquility and religious contemplations.— Gt. Har. Vol. 2, p. 313.

When the heavens are tranquil and the vesper star is seen above the clouds, . . . then the mind sees burning thoughts and words so eagle-like that it cannot but be exalted and serene.— Gt. Har. Vol. 2, p. 312.

THOUGHTS.

In great and good minds all thoughts are harmonious and meek; but the thoughts of small minds fret and strut like puppets in a show-man's box.— Penetralia, p. 10.

TRANQUILITY.

All spiritual tranquility is founded upon immortal realities. Loveliest and holiest moments are those which lift our souls as the sun and moon lift the waves of the great seas. — Beyond the Valley, p. 385.

TRUTH.

Whatsoever a man discovers in the eternal universe, it is but a reflection and correspondence of that which, germinally, lives within him, thus demonstrating that *truth* is that Principle in the presence of which *nature*, *reason*, and *intuition* harmonize and agree, and rejoice together as loving angels of God. — Gt. Har. Vol. 5, p. 32.

THOUGHT.

The influence of pure thought is like the breath of heaven upon flowers; while low thoughts fall like the vapors of pestilence. They blast the beautiful like shafts of lightning.— Answers to Questions, p. 97.

TRUTH.

That mind which loves truth more than any other thing is clothed in the Armor of Heaven; and that mind which comprehends truth is intimately allied to God, being well nigh omnipotent.— Inner Life, p. 42.

TEMPERANCE.

All excess is vicious. He who wishes to bless himself, the world by example, and posterity by the transmission of healthy qualities and noble characteristics, should be temperate in all things. The luxury of health is superior to the luxury of any habit.— Gt. Har. Vol. 4, p. 153.

THOUGHT.

Earth can forge no chains whereby to fetter human thought.— Gt. Har. Vol. 2, p. 255.

TEMPERANCE.

Temperance in all things is the only "straight and narrow way" that leads to the heaven of mental happiness.— Gt. Har. Vol. 2, p. 326.

TRUTH.

Churches, sects, creeds,— what atoms they appear! How immense is God,— rather, I would say, how omnipresent and omnipotent is *intelligent and loving truth.*— Gt. Har. Vol. 4, p. 287.

THINKERS.

A whole mind is in tune with Nature; a harmonious mind is in tune with Reason; a spiritual mind is in tune with Intuition; and such, in the true definition, is a harmonial Thinker.— Gt. Har. Vol. 5, p. 32.

TRUTH.

Truth is exactitude and completeness of representation.— Gt. Har. Vol. 5, p. 183.

TIDES.

The tides of Truth will continue to rise higher and higher, and will increase in strength and majesty as they roll forward.— Gt. Har. Vol. 3, p. 149.

THOUGHTS.

Thoughts are but Ideas in motion, and they differ from the essence which is moved as much and widely as waves differ from the water beneath them.— Gt. Har. Vol. 5, p. 62.

TEMPERANCE.

"Temperance in all things" giveth into man's possession the whole universe, whereby his soul is saved and not lost. The healthy soul enjoyeth all things.— Gt. Har. Vol. 5, p. 112.

TRUTH.

Truth is the golden door of entrance to the human heart.— Answers to Questions, p. 10.

THOUGHT.

The swinging censer of Thought flings fragrant fertilizations upon every intellect.—Gt. Har.   Vol. 5, p. 200.

TIME.

Time wasteth the blackest body of error, as rain dissolveth the hardest stratum of granite; but the spirit of truth, like the sun of heaven, is positive and imperishable.— Answers to Questions, p. 370.

TOMORROW.

Your progress and future happiness depend wholly upon the use you make of the eternal Now. . . . We must be right in heart and head *today* in order to secure a happy tomorrow.— Gt. Har.   Vol. 3, p. 362.

TRUTHS.

Truths that are unsought, or sought for their own sake, are pure and elevating to the aspiring soul.— Gt. Har. Vol. 1, p. 240.

THOUGHTS.

The Laws of Nature, which are God's Thoughts, never cease to *guide, guard, protect,* and *exercise justice.*— Gt. Har. Vol. 1, p. 145.

TYPES.

If you desire mental improvement, then improve your mental types and symbols. Obtain a knowledge of good works and deeds, as tools, with which to think.— Penetralia, p. 442.

TESTIMONY.

Beware of superficial testimony, external appearances, visible, tangible, sensuous evidences, because such are invariably liable to deceive, and are ofttimes unrighteous.— Nat. Div. Rev., p. 529.

TEMPTATION.

The light of truth will always guide the willing, faithful soul through every temptation.— Eth. of Conj. Love, p. 133.

THINKERS.

The true thinker is always enabled to see that a *man's God is the largest statement of the man himself.*— Answers to Questions, p. 19.

TRUTH.

With the free, heaven-bound soul the truth is precious wherever found, . . . and perfect love for truth casteth out all fear of error.— Gt. Har. Vol. 2, p. 396.

TONES.

Tones which vibrate within, upon the spirits' living chords, are echoed throughout the spirits' habitation. There is a mighty power in sound to soothe or to disturb.— Gt. Har. Vol. 1, p. 82.

TIME.

Time is a fine comb, and Progress is the strong iron hand that grasps it,—drawing it through all parts of the head of humanity; and it will comb it clean!—Thoughts on Religion, p. 615.

THEOLOGIANS.

In order that a man may be properly termed a theologian, he should take his text in the universal book of Nature; and his sanctuary should be the expanded earth and the unfolded heavens.—Nat. Div. Rev., p. 507.

TEMPLE.

We have only as yet entered the *vestibule* that introduces the mind into the great Temple of divine Truth, whose foundation is in the depths of the universe, whose immensity fills all space, and whose aspiring domes are lost in the heights of infinity.—Nat. Div. Rev., p. 665.

TEMPTATION.

A man must *feel*, as well as know, that it is wrong to commit certain crimes before he experiences the ability to withstand temptation.— Gt. Har. Vol. 4, p. 173.

TRUTHFULNESS.

So far as one's self-hood is involved, it is of the holiest importance that the *idea* "absolute truthfulness" should be the sole effort and perpetual prayer.— Gt. Har. Vol. 5, p. 109.

U.

UNITY.

The sea is not more true to its tide than is human life to the spirit of God. The crash and the blast of battle, like the song and dance of joy, are in harmony with the Infinite life.— Answers to Questions, p. 369.

USE.

The ultimate *Use* of Nature is to *individu-alize* and *immortalize* the human spiritual principle.— Gt. Har. Vol. 1, p. 20.

UNSELFISHNESS.

Live to make *others* better, and you will make yourself rounder, sweeter, more effect-ive in all you do, . . . and a beautiful warmth will pervade your home, . . . and noble beings will associate with you wherever you mingle wisely and lovingly with your fellowmen.— Phil. of Spir. Inter., p. 360.

UNFOLDMENT.

Just in proportion as we unfold the sensi-bilities of our minds, and arrange all the dis-cordant elements of our being into a musically harmonious order, will the joy, and light, and wisdom of the higher spheres flow in and convert us more completely into the heavenly image.— Gt. Har. Vol. 3, p. 216.

ULTIMATES.

Every material and spiritual element is being constantly ultimated intó immortalized spiritual principles.— Gt. Har. Vol. 2, p. 333.

UNCHARITABLENESS.

Let kinduess pervade your whole nature; but uncharitableness should never invade the inward sanctuary.— Gt. Har. Vol. 1, p. 434.

UNFOLDMENT.

Let thy wisdom be unfolded, and from its depths will spring the holy and beautiful truths of intuition,— the light of the inner world.— Gt. Har. Vol. 2, p. 70.

UNIVERSES.

The universe is the harp of all the impersonal principles; the silver-tongued trumpet for the use of all the gods; the perfect-toned organ played by the Eternal Master of all grand music.— Heavenly Home, p. 108.

USES.

There is nothing existing without embodying divine ideas and subserving eternal uses.— Penetralia, p. 115.

ULTIMATES.

Man, the ultimate of stupendous creations, and the germ of celestial seraphs. . . . He stands as Nature's masterpiece.— Gt. Har. Vol. 1, p. 213.

UNFOLDINGS.

Nothing is useless; for that which appears gross and imperfect is in reality the only substantial source of subsequent unfoldings.— Nat. Div. Rev., p. 324.

UNRIGHTEOUSNESS.

All evil will be subdued and banished by the ultimate triumph of those principles that are good, *divine*, and unchangeable, and unrighteousness shall be no more.— Gt. Har. Vol. 2, p. 43.

ULTIMATES.

The Great Positive Mind, as a *Cause*, develops Nature as an *Effect*, to produce the human *Spirit* as an ultimate.— Gt. Har. Vol. 2, p. 304.

USE.

Use is the central and foundation attribute of *Wisdom.* . . . Use enables the mind to place a true estimation on everything.— Gt. Har. Vol. 2, p. 147.

ULTIMATES.

The ultimate object of Nature is most beneficently, affectionately, and wisely to bring forth that seedling called the human organization.— Gt. Har.   Vol. 5, p. 371.

UNFOLDMENT.

Human minds, like trees, grow large and beautiful; or, like trees, sometimes remain small and deformed; strictly in accordance with their origin and subsequent situation.— Gt. Har.   Vol. 4, p. 54.

UNITY.

Truth is the immutable and eternal integrity of the Infinite Parents. He who lives and speaks in harmony with this integrity lives and speaks in unity with the unchangeable will and love of God.— Beyond the Valley, p. 255.

V.

VITALITY.

Vitality is a part of the Divine Mind associated *with*, and specifically acting *upon*, organized matter.— Gt. Har. Vol. 1, p. 46.

VIRTUOUSNESS.

The quicker we all abandon vices and practice virtues the more certain are we of obtaining that happiness and joy of mind which the world can neither give nor take away.— Har. Man, p. 147.

VICTORY.

There is a law of Justice which evermore overcomes evil with good.—Inner Life, p. 164.

VIOLATIONS.

The moral laws of the eternally just Father and Mother will hold unpardonably responsible every person and every sect who violates the sovereign principles of harmony.— Temple, p. 215.

VITALITY.

Nothing which manifests life and animation is without functions; and there is nothing which is not impregnated with the Eternal Spirit of all life and vitality.— Gt. Har. Vol. 2, p. 303.

VIRTUE.

Be natural, thoroughly honest, and full of integrity; then virtue's influence will always flow out from you, healing the spirits of those who are crushed by misfortune and sorrow. —Hist. and Phil. of Evil, p. 234.

VIRTUOUSNESS.

Really true and really virtuous people have the least to say about either their truthfulness or their integrity.— Temple, p. 443.

VENERATION.

Raise your thoughts to Him whose essence is love, and whose wisdom is universal justice, benevolence, and reciprocation.— Nat. Div. Rev., p. 707.

VARIETY.

Intrinsically and essentially there is no difference between human beings. All visible inequality and variety arise from different combinations of the same powers and attributes.— Har. Man, p. 154.

VISITANTS.

The sweet, mournful tones of the æolian harp, when breathed upon by the midnight wind, sound not more attractive and holy than do the whisperings of gentle visitants from other spheres.— Answers to Questions, p. 57.

W.

WANDERING.

He who searches Nature searches the gospel of God; while he who wanders from the laws and harmonies of Nature wanders from the paths and joys of the Infinite.— Inner Life, p. 44.

WISDOM.

The *true* Savior . . . is Wisdom, the embodiment and image of universal Harmony, and the ever-blooming flower of the Divine Mind.— Gt. Har.   Vol. 1, p. 453.

Wisdom, when worked out in universal society, will be the fullest realization of the " kingdom of heaven and its righteousness " ever prayed for or anticipated by *Man.*— Gt. Har.   Vol. 1, p. 454.

WISDOM.

Wisdom is greater than knowledge. The former discerns interior truths; the latter gathers external facts.— Gt. Har. Vol. 5, p. 417.

The best preventive of superstition is *Wisdom*. If you would become acquainted with your only Savior, and have anxiety to fall affectionately and confidingly at his feet, go into the presence of *Wisdom*. The most radiant angel in the chamber of the soul is *Wisdom*. His glory gleams through the infinite Palace of Truth. His young, unimpassioned bosom burns only with the immortal fires of love divine, and the voice of his words blends with the star-cadence of immensity, the bewildering music whereof surmounts the ever-upswelling crests of the eternal ocean of Principles, and fills the hushed and listening universe of intelligence with joy and hope and aspirations unutterable.— Gt. Har. Vol. 5, p. 124.

WOMAN.

Woman will inevitably develop the world. — Gt. Har. Vol. 2, p. 187.

The female spirit is a beautiful combination of immortal springs and affections.— Gt. Har. Vol. 2, p. 186.

Woman builds the foundation walls of society, . . . therefore she needs to be educated in the peculiarities of her position.— Gt. Har. Vol. 2, p. 193.

The harmonious proportions of humanity's future structure will depend entirely upon the education and elevation of the female master-builders.— Gt. Har. Vol. 2, p. 192.

All the heroes, poets, artists, philosophers, and theologians that ever moved upon the earth were put in possession of their various maxims and attributes mainly by woman.— Gt. Har. Vol. 2, p. 187.

WORTH.

All spirit and matter, all objects of thought, all thinking things, are partakers of each other's worth and nature.—Inner Life, p. 145.

WOMAN.

Woman wields the Archimedian lever, whose fulcrum is childhood, whose length is all time, whose weight is the world, whose sweep is eternity.—Gt. Har. Vol. 4, p. 257.

WEALTH.

Human souls will accumulate *spiritual substance*, obtain the real elements of mental nutrition, in strict harmony with their individual aspirations. Those who aspire to love will grow spiritually wealthy in love; those who aspire after knowledge will grow rich in the memory of facts and things; those who aspire unto Wisdom will increase in the perception and enjoyment of Principles and Generalizations.—Gt. Har. Vol. 4, p. 55.

WAR.

War is the production of the cellar-kitchen of human nationality and progress. It never comes from the upper chambers in the temple of human growth.— Phil. of Spir. Inter., p. 346.

WHOLENESS.

Nature is the *Wholeness* of all things and principles, the *Alpha* and *Omega*, the beginning and the end, the substantial and the centrestantial, matter and mind, God clothed and God unclothed, the boundless and indestructible entireness.— Gt. Har. Vol. 5, p. 31.

WEAKNESS.

The man who needs a Church, or the woman who needs a Minister, or the bishop who needs a Bible, or the religionist whose feeble faith needs the bolster of a Miracle, is not born again. Such may have the form — the signs and symbols — but not the spirit of Truth.— Free Thoughts, p. 147.

WONDERS.

It is no more wonderful that a man lives after death than that he lives after his birth. — Diakka, p. 92.

WISDOM.

Wisdom is the heart's prime minister,— the *flower* of the inward consciousness.— Gt. Har. Vol. 3, p. 109.

WEALTH.

One day material wealth will not be fashionable; but, instead, he will be most popular who is fraternal and harmonious.— Penetralia, p. 362.

WORSHIP.

True worship is an involuntary act of the inmost affections. . . . Worship of the Supreme Spirit of the Universe is possible only to those who feel, and are, therefore, powerfully attracted toward the sacred essence of the Infinite Love.— Fountain, p. 162.

WORSHIP.

The truest family worship is daily effort to establish complete integral unity and happiness.— Answers to Questions, p. 114.

WICKEDNESS.

The innate *divineness* of the spirit of man prohibits the possibility of *spiritual* wickedness or unrighteousness.— Nat. Div. Rev., p. 413.

WORDS.

God's words are fleeting things to the soul ; to the spirit they impart the imperishable realities of eternal life.— Beyond the Valley, p. 388.

WILL.

If you would know the full happiness of the harmonial angels, let your will do only what is requested by your highest affections, and only what is approved by the reflections of your highest Reason.—Heavenly Home, p. 28.

WISDOM.

Our Redeemer is Wisdom, whose ways are pleasant; whose paths are peace ; whose heart is Mother nature ; whose head is Father God ; who saves the whole world with an everlasting salvation. Truth, Love, Justice, Wisdom, — each an angel of life, light, and happiness. Let us strive to communicate with them; let us listen reverently to no other voices ; let us obey no other authorities.— Fountain, p. 231.

INDEX.

List of the Complete Works of

ANDREW JACKSON DAVIS.

Twenty-nine Volumes, all uniform, printed in good style, and neatly bound in cloth.

For sale, wholesale and retail, by the publishers, COLBY & RICH, corner Bosworth and Province Sts., Boston, Mass.

☞ These works form a library in themselves. They are remarkable from every point of view,— in the comprehensiveness of their scope, in their penetration and clear analysis, in their richness of language, and in the depth of insight to which they conduct the reader.

Principles of Nature: Her Divine Revelations, and a Voice to Mankind.

(In three parts.) Fortieth edition, just published, with a likeness of the author, and containing a family record for marriages, births, and deaths. This is the first and most comprehensive volume of Mr. Davis, comprising the basis and ample outline of the Harmonial Philosophy. Its claims are confessedly of the most startling character, and its professed disclosures, with the phenomena attending them, are in some respects unparalleled in the history of psychology. $3.50
Red line edition, full morocco, levant, gilt. . . 12.00

Great Harmony: Being a Philosophical Revelation of the Natural, Spiritual, and Celestial Universe. In Five Vols.

Vol. I. THE PHYSICIAN. In this volume is considered the Origin and Nature of Man ; the Philosophy of Health, Disease, Sleep, Death, Psychology, and Healing. . . 1.50
Vol. II. THE TEACHER. In this volume is presented the new and wonderful principles of " Spirit and its Culture "; also, a comprehensive and systematic argument on the " Existence of God." 1.50
Vol. III. THE SEER. This volume is composed of twenty-seven Lectures on every phase of Magnetism and

1

Clairvoyance. The whole ground of Psychology and Inspiration is examined in detail. 1.50
Vol. IV. THE REFORMER. This volume is devoted to the consideration of "Physiological Vices and Virtues, and the Seven Phases of Marriage." New views of marriage and parentage ; woman's rights and wrongs ; transient and permanent marriage ; temperaments ; the rights and wrongs of divorce, etc. 1.50
Vol. V. THE THINKER. The most comprehensive volume of the series. The Pantheon of Progress ; The Origin of Life, and the Law of Immortality. No book extant contains any such argument as that running through the chapters on "Immortality," or any such metaphysics as distinguish the "Pantheon of Progress." 1.50

Magic Staff. An Autobiography of Andrew Jackson Davis.

A well-authenticated history of the domestic, social, physical, and literary career of the author, with his remarkable experiences as a Clairvoyant and Seer. The work is very attractive to children and young minds, and to all new beginners in these new truths. 1.75

A Stellar Key to the Summer-Land.

Illustrated with Diagrams and Engravings of Celestial Scenery. The description of physical scenery and the constitution of the Summer-Land, its location, and domestic life in the spheres, are new and wonderfully interesting. 75
Paper covers. 50

Views of Our Heavenly Home.

A sequel to "A Stellar Key." Illustrated. Among the contents are statements in regard to "individual occupation," and "progress after death," "eating and drinking in the spirit-life," "disappearance of the bodily organs at death," "domestic enjoyments and true conjugal unions," "origin of the doctrine of the devil," etc. Cloth. 75
Paper covers. 50

Arabula; or, The Divine Guest.

Pre-eminently a religious and spiritual volume. "I am Arabula ; I am the light of the world ; he that followeth me shall have light and life ; he that loveth me keepeth my

2

commandments." To some extent, a continuation of the author's autobiography. Also, containing a new collection of Living Gospels from Ancient and Modern Saints.   1.50

Approaching Crisis; or, Truth vs. Theology.

This is a close and searching criticism of the Bible, Nature, Religion, Skepticism, and the Supernatural. It is affirmed by many of the most careful readers of Mr. Davis's works that the best explanation of the " Origin of Evil " is to be found in this volume. 1.00

Answers to Ever-Recurring Questions from the People.

(A sequel to " Penetralia.") These answers comprise a wide range of subjects, embracing points of peculiar interest and the highest value, connected with the Harmonial Philosophy and Practical Reform. 1.50

Children's Progressive Lyceum.

A Manual, with Directions for the Organization and Management of Sunday Schools, adapted to the Bodies and Minds of the Young, and containing Rules, Methods, Exercises, Marches, Lessons, Questions and Answers, Invocations, Silver-Chain Recitations, Hymns, and Songs.   . 50
Twelve copies. 5.50

History and Philosophy of Evil.

With Suggestions for More Ennobling Institutions, and Philosophical Systems of Education. The whole question of Evil — individual, social, national, and general — is fully analyzed and answered. Cloth. 75
Paper covers. 50

Death and After-Life.

Thousands upon thousands of this wonderful little volume have been sold and read. Some idea of this little volume may be gained from the following table of contents : 1. Death and the After-Life ; 2. Scenes in the Summer-Land ; 3. Society in the Summer-Land ; 4. Social Centres in the Summer-Land; 5. Winter-Land and Summer-Land; 6. Language and Life in Summer-Land ; 7. Material Work for Spiritual Workers ; 8. Ultimates in the Summer-Land ; 9. Voice from James Victor Wilson. Cloth. 75
Paper covers. 50

3

Harbinger of Health; containing Medical Prescriptions for the Human Body and Mind.

It imparts knowledge whereby any individual may be greatly assisted in resisting and overcoming the assaults of disease, and enjoying uninterrupted good health. The first volume of the "Harmonia," "The Physician," this work, "The Harbinger of Health," and "Mental Disorders, or Diseases of the Brain and Nerves,"—these three books alone make a reliable medical library for a family, or a student of Philosophy and the Science of Life and Health. 1.50

Harmonial Man; or, Thoughts for the Age.

Designed to enlarge man's views concerning the political and ecclesiastical condition of America, and to point out the paths of reform ; also considers scientifically the meteoric laws, and the philosophy of controlling rain. Cloth. 75
Paper covers. 50

Events in the Life of a Seer. (MEMORANDA.)

Embracing Authentic Facts, Visions, Impressions, Discoveries in Magnetism, Clairvoyance, and Spiritualism. Also, Quotations from the Opposition. With an Appendix, containing Zschokke's Great Story, "Hortensia," vividly portraying the difference between the Ordinary State and that of Clairvoyance. 1.50

The Diakka, and their Earthly Victims.

Being an explanation of much that is false and repulsive in Spiritualism, embodying a most important recent interview with James Victor Wilson, who is a resident of the Summer-Land. Cloth. 50
Paper covers. 25

Philosophy of Special Providences.

The author's "vision" of the harmonious works of the Creator is fully given in this bright little book. He illustrates the chain of special providences which mankind attribute to the direct acts of the Deity. Cloth. . . . 50
Paper covers. 30

Free Thoughts Concerning Religion.

Containing the most radical thoughts, critical and explanatory, concerning popular religious ideas, their origin,

4

imperfections, and the changes that must come over the popular church doctrines. Cloth. 75
    Paper covers. 50

Penetralia. Containing Harmonial Answers.

This work at the time was styled by the author's readers "the wisest book" from his pen. Some of the chapters are overflowing with rare and glorious revelations of the realities of the world beyond the grave. 1.75

Philosophy of Spiritual Intercourse.

Contains an account of the very wonderful Spiritual Developments at the house of Rev. Dr. Phelps, Stratford, Conn., and similar cases in all parts of the country. This volume is the first from the author directly on the subject of "Spiritualism," and its positions and principles and good counsels have stood the test of thirty years of the most varied and searching experiences by thousands of mediums and investigators. 1.25

The Inner Life; or, Spirit Mysteries Explained.

This is a sequel to "Philosophy of Spiritual Intercourse," recently revised and enlarged. It presents a compend of the Harmonial Philosophy of "Spiritualism," with illustrative facts of spiritual intercourse, both ancient and modern, and a thorough and original treatise upon the laws and conditions of mediumship. Cloth. 1.50

The Temple; or, Diseases of the Brain and Nerves.

Developing the Origin and Philosophy of Mania, Insanity, and Crime ; with full directions and Prescriptions for their Treatment and Cure. This large, handsome volume treats the Question of Insanity and Crime from a Spiritual and Psychological standpoint ; with an Original Frontispiece illustrative of "Mother Nature Casting (D)evils Out of Her Children." Cloth. 1.50

The Fountain; with Jets of New Meanings.

This attractive little volume is teeming with thoughts for men and pictures for children. The young as well as the old can read it and study its lessons and illustrations with ever-increasing pleasure and profit. It covers a wide range of topics. Cloth. 1.00

Tale of a Physician ; or, the Seeds and Fruits of Crime.

A wonderfully interesting book. Society is unveiled. This book is as attractive as the most thrilling romance, and yet it explains the producing causes of theft, murder, suicide, fœticide, infanticide, and the other nameless evils which afflict society and alarm all the friends of humanity. Cloth. 1.00

The Genesis and Ethics of Conjugal Love.

This new book treats of all the delicate and important questions involved in conjugal love ; is straightforward, unmistakably emphatic, and perfectly explicit and plain in every vital particular. Cloth. 75

Beyond the Valley ; A Sequel to the Magic Staff; An Autobiography of Andrew Jackson Davis. Six Beautiful Illustrations.

The numerous friends of Mr. Davis will hail this fresh and handsome volume with delight. He has not written anything more timely and important for many years. The history of his life is the history of a spirit, as unfolded and influenced by guardian angels, amid the circumstances and entanglements of human society. His chapters are pathetic and authentic records of events and scenes in his private and public career, beginning where the "Magic Staff" ends, and bringing his psychological and private experiences truthfully up to the present day. 1.50

☞ Any book named in the foregoing list that may be desired, or the complete works to one address, will be forwarded promptly, by mail or express, on receipt of price. [Nearly all the foregoing have been translated, and can be obtained in the German language, by addressing Wilhelm Besser, publisher, No. 2 Market Street, Leipzig, Germany.]

Price of the Complete Works of A. J. Davis, all firmly and uniformly bound in black cloth, $30.

These volumes may be obtained by addressing the publishers of the *Banner of Light*, COLBY & RICH, Boston, Mass. In remitting by post-office money-order, or otherwise, please make it payable to Colby & Rich. The trade supplied on liberal terms.

www.ingramcontent.com/pod-product-compliance
Lightning Source LLC
Chambersburg PA
CBHW020604030726
47497CB00007B/2076